JUDGE NOT MY SINS

Also By Stuart James

Frisco Flat
Bucks County Report

JUDGE NOT MY SINS

STUART JAMES

CUTTING EDGE

ISBN-13: 978-1-952138-73-7

Published by

CUTTING EDGE

PO Box 8212
Calabasas, CA 91372
www.cuttingedgebooks.com

If it was love, it was also fear, and we might have huddled behind a rock while the night wind devoured the plain.

"Save me," I heard her cry.

—Norman Mailer
Barbary Shore

PROLOGUE

This is David Markam.

A young man of 34, he walks along 31st Street in New York City. He has just left a cab at the corner of Third Avenue. It is a spring night and he wears a light trench coat. He has a mustache outstanding amidst gaunt features, and a pipe juts from his outthrust jaw.

The girl with her hand folded into the crook of his elbow is blonde, four inches below David's six feet height, and easily the most beautiful girl he has ever seen.

"This is it," the girl said, tugging his arm.

David stopped, surveyed the brick building with a quick glance. The girl had loosened her grip and was rummaging in her purse for a key.

"Damn," she muttered, "I can never find anything."

David peered closely at a brass plate next to the door of the building. He read the two names to himself. "Is this an office building?" he asked.

The girl looked up from her purse, followed his eyes to the brass plate. "Photographers," she said. "I have the top floor." She returned to her search.

David watched her. She was intent on her task, muttering, shuffling the contents of the overburdened purse. He wondered if he was going to make love to her. It was obvious that she was going to ask him in. He wanted to make love to her. Well, that was nothing new. She was a woman. She was beautiful. And he couldn't remember her name. The perfect ingredients for wanting to make love to a woman.

"Here it is," she said, lifting the key between her fingers, and flashing a small smile of triumph.

David took the key from her, climbed the two steps, inserted it in the lock. He opened the door and she stepped in ahead of him. He followed, let the door close.

The girl started up the stairway and David followed. For the first time he saw the fine lines of her full calves, the slim ankles. She wore a raincoat that rustled against her legs. She had worn the raincoat since he had first met her, and it was difficult to tell about her body, but it looked good, and the face was perfect—angelic.

"Wait," the girl said. She had reached the first landing and turned. She stopped David's approach, resting her hands on his shoulders. Her expression was suddenly pensive. "Are you certain you want to do this?"

"Do what?"

"Come with me like this."

"Why not? What's wrong with it?"

She bit down on her lower lip and stared at him with luminous blue eyes for a long moment. "Nothing," she said, "come along." She turned and walked along the hall, turned into the next flight of steps. David followed. At the next landing she stopped and turned again. "I don't know," she said.

"About what?" David asked, beginning to weary of whatever it was she didn't know.

"I'm afraid you'll be in love with me," she said.

"Try me," he said.

"I mean it," she said. "I wouldn't like that."

"I promise not to."

She chewed her lips and her eyes narrowed thoughtfully, as though she were seriously considering the validity of his promise. "I'm certain that you will," she said.

David sighed. Just his luck. A beautiful girl. She asks him home. And she has to be a nut. "Scout's honor," he said.

The eyes changed. They were smiling, and she asked, "Were you a scout?"

"No," he said.

"Then why did you say . . ."

"Are we going to stand here and talk all night?"

She caught her breath, then she smiled, and David's pulse quickened as he was caught in the radiance of the most beguiling smile he had ever seen. "I'm sorry," she said. She turned again, and went heel-clacking along the hall and into the next flight of stairs.

"Another flight?" David asked.

"This is the last," she said.

"Point of no return," David said.

She stopped suddenly and whirled. "Why did you say that?"

"I . . . uh . . ." There didn't seem to be a reasonable explanation. "I don't know," he said. "It just seemed like something to say. I mean, after all your talk about . . ."

"You're making fun of me." The eyes had changed again and now they were sparkling with quick anger.

Damn, David thought, and we're not even up the steps yet. "Look," he said, wearily, "I'm not making fun of you. I said it because I think it's idiotic to think I'm going to fall in love with you just because I'm going to your apartment. I don't even know you."

The anger subsided. "I'm sorry," she said, her voice subdued. "I guess I'm nervous." She turned again and started up the stairs. David shook his head and followed.

They reached her door, the only one at the top. "Use the second key," she said.

David fumbled, trying to remember which key he used in the downstairs door. She pointed. He put the key in the lock and began to open the door. A dog snarled, startling him.

"Fang!" the girl snapped. The growling ceased, and David opened the door. The girl stepped in ahead of him, pushing the large Doberman ahead of her. The dog was black, lithe, powerfully muscular. He danced backwards, nuzzling at the girl's hand, making whimpering sounds.

David closed the door and followed her along the short hall. He gazed at the dog, clucking his tongue against the roof of his mouth. Nothing like being well-chaperoned, he thought.

The hallway opened onto a huge rectangular living room. The floor was black, the walls white. It was psuedo-Japanese with low tables, cushions on the floor, a white screen across the far end of the room. One wall was white brick with an austere fireplace. There was a long, black, ornately carved chest against one wall. Lights were suspended from the ceiling and contained in large, balloon-like Japanese lanterns. It was unusual for a New York apartment, but effective.

"Quite a room," David said.

"I like space," she said, shrugging out of her coat, and draping it over the chest.

"You've certainly got it," David said. He was looking about the room, but now his gaze stopped on the girl.

"You'll have to see the rest of the place," she said. "There are three more rooms."

David was only half listening. He stared at her. If it was possible to fall in love with a body, the girl's fears were justified. She wore a black dress that clung to her, a startling contrast to the corn-colored hair. Everything about her seemed to be in the right proportion. She was tall, her neck was arched, perfectly formed; the undulations of slightly sloping shoulders, high breasts, waist and hips were distinctly feminine, womanly; a mating of sophistication and earthiness.

She had stopped speaking and when David looked up at her face the eyes were shaded with sadness, the expression of the mouth wistful. "You're staring at me," she said.

"I'm sorry," he said. "It's just that I hadn't seen you before. You're beautiful."

"Don't," she said, a slight note of pleading in her voice.

"What?"

"Don't be like other men."

"I'm a man," he said. "That's all I am. I was just looking at a beautiful woman."

She turned slowly and walked the length of the long room. She slid a portion of the screen aside, exposing a large window that looked out upon the lighted skyline of New York. She stood with her back to David. The room was charged with silence. The black dog lay in the middle of the room, relaxed and tense at the same time. Its head was arched, and the wary eyes moved between David and the girl. David stood at the far end of the room, near the small kitchenette, watching the girl, listening to the silence. When she spoke her voice was distant. It was almost a whisper, but its resonance carried and filled the room. It had a dirge-like quality, a voice speaking from the lonely depths of the soul. "I wanted to be ugly," she said. "I wanted to be ugly on the outside. I wanted a mask to cover beauty; to have all the beauty inside where people could not see it. I wanted it so that one day a man would feel the beauty and he would be strong enough and tender enough to accept the beauty and his love would transform the ugliness to loveliness, but for his eyes alone."

She stopped speaking. The plaintive anguish of her voice seemed to echo in the still room. David glanced at the dog and it seemed as though the animal were listening and understanding. It was a strange experience, and David found that he was conscious of his breathing, being careful of it lest he make a sound.

"Once," the girl said, starting again, "I thought about using acid on my face."

David waited, but she said no more. He was uncomfortable, nervous, and he had the feeling that he should not speak, that if he once mouthed words he would suddenly be enmeshed in an emotional web. He sensed that a door had been opened to him, and beyond the threshold was a frightening darkness, and he felt that once he stepped into the void the door would close behind him, never to open again. "Why didn't you?" he asked.

The girl stiffened and turned. Her eyes blinked as though she was only now aware of his presence, as though she had just returned from some distance place. One hand fluttered to her throat. She smiled suddenly, breaking the reverie. She slid the screen back into place and started across the room. "Let me show you the rest of the place," she said.

David scowled, his curiosity unabated, but the mood of the moment was gone. She stopped next to him, still smiling, and raised a finger to his brow. "Don't look so fierce," she said. David lifted a hand to stay her, the words forming to question her, but she had already moved away, her step light, her mood changed. He dropped his hand and shook his head. Then he followed her.

They entered a room that was as large as the living room and painted the same colors. It contained a desk, a typewriter, a filing cabinet. Nothing else. It was bare, austere, businesslike.

"This your office?" David asked.

"Yes."

"You're in business?"

"I was," she said. "I gave it up."

"What business?"

"I was a manufacturer's representative," she said. "I bought aircraft parts. Very dull."

"What do you do now?"

"Nothing."

David was about to ask further questions, but she was gone again. He bit down on the words and followed.

The next room was smaller and it was impossible to get past the door. The walls were painted a dull, lusterless gray. It was a storage room, jammed with a collection of chairs and tables, lamps, boxes of books, straw hats, paintings, a seedy racoon coat, suitcases, paper boxes. It was a disordered clutter. Everything seemed to have been hastily thrown in from the doorway.

"I hate this room," she said. She turned away quickly and David followed her back to the living room. She opened a door to the right of the kitchenette and ushered him into the bedroom. It was a room slightly larger than the storeroom. The walls were pastel green, the ceiling a warm shade of peach. The wall-to-wall carpet was beige. There was a tall chest of drawers, a large dresser with mirror, two wing-back chairs. The bed was large and the headboard was a bookcase. The furniture was in dark maple and the chairs were covered with a cotton print material.

David was startled by the room. It had a warmth, a lived-in quality that was lacking in the rest of the apartment. He turned to the girl and caught his breath. Except for the obvious physical similarity, he was looking at a different person. She was relaxed. She moved across the room as though she belonged, as though she had just arrived home from some far place, and she exuded a radiance that complemented the decor of the room.

Standing in the middle of the room, David watched her turn and come towards him. She stopped before him, stood there saying nothing, her arms at her sides, looking into him. He felt his nerves tremble. He wanted to reach for her, but he was afraid to break the mood. The beauty, the warmth of her, created a constriction in his chest. He looked back into her eyes and he saw longing there, saw the bottomless depths of loneliness.

She rose on her toes and leaned forward. Her lips grazed his for an instant, then she moved away. It was the mere suggestion of a kiss, but his heart leaped and he felt the sudden wave of emotion strike the deep core of his senses. She turned and moved away, going to the dresser to turn on the radio. He watched her, a scowl marring his forehead, the deep furrows gathering at the bridge of his nose.

He saw again the odd decor of the entire apartment and knew that he was looking at the girl. The austerity of the living room was the face she turned to the world, impersonal, unemotional, devoid of feeling. The office was even colder. The drab gray of the storeroom was her past, all the clutter of what she had known and cast away from her. The bedroom was the woman, the beauty, the warmth, the love that crouched, waiting with the trembling rabbit-heart of the woman-within-woman.

Static, the dissonance of voices hastily changed, then music came from the radio. She flicked a switch that transferred the speaker to the living room, turned the volume down.

"Coffee?" she said, turning to face him.

"I'd like that," he said.

"Good, I'll make it." She walked past him and through the door. He followed, closing the door after him.

She watched him close the door and the smile left her face. She stood at the end of the bar which separated the kitchenette from the room. "Now *you're* afraid," she said.

David glanced back at the door, then at the girl. He hesitated a moment. He came and perched on one of the stools facing the bar. "Not afraid," he said. "It's something different. I'm not certain exactly what, but it is more like caution. I mean I've never met anyone quite like you, and I . . ."

"You think I'm crazy?"

She had interrupted his train of thought and he had to pause a moment to consider her new question. "No, I don't," he said. "Different, but not crazy."

"Do you want to make love to me?"

He looked hard at her. Her questions came too fast. It was not repartee, there was no flippancy to it, and he knew that he had to answer with serious conviction and honesty, knew that she expected it. He swallowed and one hand gripped the other.

"I'd like some coffee," he said.

She smiled, then reached under the counter for a pan and moved to the sink and the water tap. She filled the pan and placed it on the stove. She came back to the counter and stood opposite him.

"You promised not to love me," she said.

"I know." His eyes dropped to his hands. "I. . ." He paused. It was difficult, confusing. "Look," he said, lifting his head, "couldn't we talk about something else? I don't think I like this?"

"But you came here to make love to me," she said.

He stared at her with an even concentration for a long moment, then he spoke. "That's right. You were a girl. A girl I met in the night."

"And now I'm not?"

He took a deep breath and his eyes dropped again. He nodded. "And now you're not," he said. He looked up at her again and there was the wistful little-girl expression again. He lifted his fist and bit on his knuckles, not taking his eyes from her face. "That's too bad, isn't it?" he said.

She nodded. She was standing with both hands touching the edge of the counter. Impulsively, David reached out and gripped her wrist. Her lips parted and her eyes flashed.

The dog came to his feet and a deep growl built in his chest. The teeth were bared and the animal was poised, taut as a bowstring.

"Down, Fang!" the girl snapped.

David released her wrist and drew his hand back. He looked at the dog, watched it settle down on the floor, embarrassed, but watchful. David turned back to the girl.

"Strange name for the dog," he said.

"Funny," she said. "Amusing funny. Nobody really expects a dog to be named Fang." She turned to the stove where the water was boiling. She turned off the gas, then brought down cups and a jar of instant coffee.

"I used to have a dog," David said. "A mongrel type dog."

"You managed to change the subject," she said.

He shrugged and smiled with a mock rueful expression, but did not answer. This was definitely not the kind of girl who spent the evening in small talk. She had a way of slicing through sham and insisting on direction. It was not evident in her appearance or in outward movement, but in conversation she was incisive and purposeful. There was an enigmatic quality to her that was disconcerting.

They drank their coffee in awkward silence. David could not speak. The subject matter was limited and he was afraid to pursue the obvious. He had the feeling, knew for some inexplicable reason, that the only thing they could talk about was each other, one in relation to the other. It was a subject that he might have entered with relish had it been with some other girl. It would have been a gambit. He knew the things to say that a girl would want to hear who needed reassurance for what was already decided in her mind. It was a game, a method of putting love-making on a civilized or intellectual basis. It was something you indulged in, regretting the shallowness in a deep recess of the mind, but admitting—and even believing—that any means justified the end. With this girl the concept of such self-deception was ludicrous.

"I think I'd better be going," David said.

The slightest suggestion of a smile passed over her face. "You're being afraid again," she said.

"Stop it!" David snapped, coming to his feet abruptly, slamming his open palm down on the counter. "Just lay off! I'm afraid. All right, I'm afraid. But don't rub it in." His facial muscles were taut and he gripped the edge of the counter, leaning towards her, the words coming fast and clipped, because he was incensed with a sudden anger. "I came up here for one thing. You know it and I know it. You were a pretty girl I met at Galligans. That's all. I figured you for a fast roll in the hay. That's all it was." His voice rose and he trembled as he spoke. "But that's not enough now. I want you, but not that way. I don't know just how, I don't really know what this is all about, but I do know that a one-night stand isn't it. You know that it's wrong and so do I. I feel it, I honest-to-God know that I ought to get out of here."

"Don't go," she said.

"Shut up! I want to finish. I feel something for you. I don't know what it is . . ."

"It's love."

". . . I said, shut up. I don't think it's love. I damn well don't know what it is, but it bothers me." His voice was tense. "It makes me afraid, I'll admit it, but don't bug me about it."

"I can tell you what it is."

"I'm leaving."

They were both silent. There was the sudden void. The background of music, the quick breathing, the expectant rustle of the dog moving on the floor.

The girl took a deep breath and bit down on her lower lip. Her eyes dropped and she swallowed. "I'll get your coat," she said.

David watched her come around the end of the counter. He relaxed, removed his hands from the counter and turned to her. She lifted the trench coat and held it up for him. He turned his back and slipped his arms into the sleeves, shrugging it up over his shoulders. He jammed his hands deep into the pockets and turned to her.

"Look," he said, "I'm sorry if I sounded like . . . well . . . you know."

"It's all right," she said. She attempted a smile, but it didn't quite form and there was a hesitant coolness in her voice.

He took a deep breath and was about to say something, somehow explain to her the way he felt, but the words did not form in his mind, and he pursed his lips and shrugged.

"If you're going to go you had better go," she said. There was a crispness to her tone.

David felt the reluctance to move, but there was also the feeling that it was the right thing to do. Why, he didn't know, but a feeling had passed between them, a rapport. It happens all the time. A man is in a room. He looks up and there is a woman. Their eyes meet and something happens. It cannot be explained, but it exists, it happens. It was like that with David. He knew that the feeling was there.

Stepping back, he took a deep breath and nodded his head. He bit his lip, then he said, hesitating over each word, "yes . . . yes . . . I . . . had better . . . I . . ."

"Please," she whispered, her voice suddenly fraught with pleading, speaking to him with the frantic loneliness of her eyes.

He clenched his teeth to stay the trembling within him. They stood in silence, separated by a veil of fear, two people poised on the brink of a crevasse, decided, but frightened of the dark void into which they knew they must plummet.

Their eyes held. She took a tentative step forward. He waited, but his eyes told her to come to him. She paused for a second that seemed interminably long, then she caught her breath, and fell against him, burrowing her face into his chest, encircling him with her arms, holding on with relief and desperation.

The gap was closed. He sighed aloud. His right hand burrowed into her hair. His left hand settled in the small of her back. He bent his face to her hair, savoring the combined scent of cologne and rain. A galaxy of emotion spun and exploded within him, and he held her tightly.

She lifted her face and tears glistened in her eyes, but her expression was happy, secure. "I don't want you to go," she whispered.

"No."

"Stay."

"Yes."

"Oh . . ." Her voice trailed off and she closed her eyes, pressing herself against him.

He lowered his lips to hers. They touched gently, a furtive brush. She did not speak, but her lips formed words against his.

"Love me." He moulded his mouth to hers and then he was lost in the cataclysm of longing. His heart thudded painfully. His nerves responded and sensation of touch, the awareness of her, spread over him. He felt with new clarity the press of her breasts against him, the frantic grip of her hands against his back, the pressure of her thighs against his. She moved her head, increasing the force of the kiss. Her hands left his back and encircled his neck. She clung to him, kissing him with new hunger. Their lips parted, teeth clicked in clumsy anxiety, then David's tongue touched hers, the contact electrifying him.

She pulled her head away. She arched against him, her head back, her eyes still closed. She moved her head from side to side. "Yes," she whispered, as though she were speaking to herself. "Yes . . . oh . . . yes." She gripped him more tightly, and her lips returned to find his and she kissed him with renewed fervor.

The dog shifted on the floor and whimpered.

She moved her lips away and the fraction of an inch separated them. "Love me," she whispered.

"I do," he said, and he tensed suddenly with the realization that he meant it, that it was madness, but that he did mean it, that he wanted her, wanted to love her, wanted her.

Her voice was a strangled plea, the voice of a small girl. "Take me to bed," she said.

He awoke in the confusion of love. The radio alarm came on and he sat up in the bed. The room was strange and dawn streamed through the window facing the street. He rubbed his eyes, listened to the street sounds of morning. He turned his head and stared down at the sleeping girl.

Her blonde hair sprawled over the pillow. She cradled the pillow with one arm and her breathing was slow and even. In sleep her expression was placid. She wore no makeup, but there were the slight traces of lipstick on the perfectly formed lips.

He felt strange, remembering what did not seem real. He took a deep breath and shook his head. He leaned forward to peer at the clock. It was early. He lay back, his hands joined behind his head. He turned and gazed at her. The light blanket and sheet were pulled up to her neck. He turned on his side, supporting his head with his right hand, and reached out to touch her with his left.

She stirred, mumbling, and he smiled. He moved closer to her and blew softly against the nape of her neck. She squirmed, moving her head. He blew again.

She was beautiful, more beautiful in the daylight. Defenseless in her sleep, angelic.

He leaned over and brushed her lips with his. He moved his hand over her waist, stroked the velvet skin. She came awake suddenly, spun about and stared at him with surprise widening her eyes. She bit down on her lower lip, as though stunned to find him there.

"Oh," she said, "you."

"You expected maybe, Lassie," he said, scowling.

She pursed her lips and her eyes smiled. "You're funny, too," she said.

"Too?"

Her head was nestled in the crook of her elbow, both imbedded in the pillow. "My funny lover," she said.

"You remember, then."

"Of course."

"Good memory?"

"Wonderful," she said, the eyes still smiling. "You look nice in bed."

"You too."

"Even in the morning?"

"Especially in the morning."

They lay facing each other, separated, but held together with their eyes. They were silent, looking, judging, then he reached out and touched her shoulder. She moved her hand from her head and covered his hand. The smile had left her eyes and now she was serious, probing his face.

"You frighten me," she said.

"Still? I thought we finished that last night."

"More than ever now," she said. "Looking at you I fall apart inside. When you touch me—" She didn't finish.

"It must be good," he said.

"You don't know me," she said.

"I will," he said.

She bit on her lip and closed her eyes as though some painful thought had just fluttered across her mind. She opened her eyes, taking a deep breath. Pulling his hand away from her arm, she moved it, turning the palm up. She brought his hand to her lips. She held it there, lingering, then she moved it down and covered her breast.

There was an element of quiet desperation in the move, and David found it vaguely disturbing.

She moved cat-like, sliding close to him. She pressed her face against his chest, moulded her body to his, holding on to him. There seemed to be more fear in the movement than passion. She clung to him as though seeking refuge, as though she was placing him between her and something beyond them both. David brought his arms about her and held her close to him. He felt the slight tremor in her body, felt it became still as she nuzzled close.

He furrowed his brow. There were so many moods to her. She smiled, laughed, then suddenly she was serious, and in the next instant she was caught in the abyss of terror. He kissed the top of her head, and she lifted her face. She was smiling again. The moment of fear had passed.

"You're very strong," she said. She squirmed against him, bringing her face to meet his. He kissed her, turning her head, pressing her into the pillow. His desire for her began to spread. He was aware of the body pressing against him, moving against him. He forgot to breathe and his eyes were closed, sharpening his sense of touch. He loved her and he wanted her. He moved his mouth from hers, gasped for breath, kissed her face, moved his lips into the hollow of her throat, savoring the lavender taste of her, moved his lips down to brush lightly over her breast. She grasped his head and pulled him into the breast-soft flesh, holding him so that he could hear the pounding of her heart.

Thigh to thigh, breast to breast, belly to belly, they became one entity, one breath-held, teeth-clenched, lip-touched being, divorced from reality, plummeted into the depth of soul. Swaying, clinging, they led each other into the beauty of love-passion, mindless of the world that moved beyond the window, creating their own world that was a galaxy of multi-colored light beating against the iris of closed eye.

They clung together even as the passion subsided and their breathing was ragged, forcing strength into dissipated muscles. They lay together for long minutes, then she said, "That's what frightens me."

"It shouldn't," he said. "It's beautiful."

"That's it!" She jerked away from him, startling him. She tossed her head and sat up. She pulled her legs up, hugging her knees. She stared out into the room. "That's exactly what's wrong."

"How can beauty be wrong?" David had twisted and he gazed at her pose, so like the classic simplicity of an Edward Weston nude, the unbroken line of back and thigh and leg.

"It's not just that," she said, "it's me. I can't love!" She spoke the words evenly and softly, but they were issued with impact, an outcry against the frustrated image of self.

David did not move or speak. He watched her face, saw the sudden despair. She closed her eyes and lowered her forehead to her knees.

"I'm not sure I understand," David said, after a long pause. "I won't try to give you a lot of crap about how I can change the way you feel." He spoke with gravity, and she lifted her face to look at him. "Something bothers you, I know that. I also know that we have found something. Even there I'm not sure what it is. I feel that I love you. I know that. I want to see you again, and I'd like you to give me the chance to be something to you." He stopped speaking and their eyes held.

She bit down on her lip and her eyes misted. "I knew it when I saw you," she said. "Later I was sure of it."

"What?"

"That you're nice," she said.

"I know some people who would argue the point," David said.

"They don't know you."

"Maybe not."

She watched him silently, then she smiled. "Go away," she said. "Get dressed and go away. I have to be alone with myself. You've gotten me confused."

Their gaze held, then David nodded. He slid from beneath the sheet, swung his legs off the bed and stood. He went to the chair where his clothes were draped. He kept his back to her as he dressed, and when he was finished he turned. "Do you want me to come back?"

She shook her head. "No," she said, "I don't want to see you again."

"You're sure?"

"Yes."

He nodded, gazed at her, then he squared his shoulders and went to the door. He stopped, looked at her again, then he opened the door and went into the living room. The black dog eyed him with suspicion, but David ignored the animal. He went along the hallway and let himself out of the apartment.

Going down the stairs he had the feeling that he was leaving something vital and precious. He shrugged, knowing that he had to go. At the bottom he paused by the three mailboxes, and it occurred to him that he had never learned her name.

Leaning over, he peered at the name on the middle box. The other two were the names of the photographers. He looked closely.

"Leslie," he said aloud. "Leslie Darrow." He rummaged in his coat for a pencil and wrote the name on the inside of a match-book cover.

Opening the door, he stepped out into the clamor of the street.

CHAPTER ONE

Who was I that morning? I asked myself the question as I walked into the morning sounds of city. Who was I? What did I think, believe, know, feel? My name was David Markam, but that was a yesterday label, a tag, the identification for a certain body of a certain size. I had a past, thirty-four years of it. But now who was I and what did I really think and where was I going?

I moved along thirty-first street with a buoyancy that I had not known since youth. It was a strange combination of feelings. Confusion and this other feeling of lightheartedness, the way I felt one time during high school when I had kissed a girl for the first time and I ran through the night, elation bursting from me, and I had to leap up and swing on the limb of a tree. Like that.

Second Avenue was spread with the bright newness of morning sun. Traffic released by a change of lights charged across the intersection, expelling grey-blue exhaust, grinding out the sounds of impatience.

I turned the corner and walked into the tide of go-to-work faces, impassive, flaccid, vacant, grim. No smiles for the workaday. Heel-stilted bouncing girls, nylon legs dropping from folds of crinoline, tight-waisted and pert-breasted; happy swinging bodies and bored last-night faces. Wide awake legs carrying sleepy bodies. Lately risen brains still fuzzily pillow held.

There was no rush for me, no determined purpose to my stride, so the morning-march went past me, broke and eddied about me as water cleaves past a rock, leaving me with the stigma of curious glance and angry glower. I was out of place. I was not office-bound, not a worker, and their eyes chastised me for my indolence.

I smiled in return. I pulled my tie loose and unbuttoned my collar. I jammed my hands deep into pockets and slouched for all their indignation. I felt good.

I had met a girl, an unusual, incredible girl, a beautiful girl. I walked the street under the bright sun with the smells of love still upon me, and I felt good.

Leslie. Her name was Leslie. I saw it on the mailbox when I left. A chance meeting in a bar. A glance, eyes meet. The moments of indecision, then the opening gambit, lighting her cigarette. A joke, a word about the weather. The hesitant gulf between man and woman, wary for fear of being rebuffed, staying the palpitating eagerness to protect the veneer ego. Her smile saying, I am willing to speak with you, and then the flow of conversation.

A pick-up in a bar. Strangers in a large, soft bed, brought together by city loneliness and the hunger for human touch. A cheap one-night grappling of sweating bodies, the casual debauch, the dregs of immorality. But then there was something new, something different. As our bodies met in passion there was an awakening, the birthing of something strange and unknown, a feeling of such depth that it defied casual explanation.

And so, as I walked the street that morning I was not the same David Markam who had climbed those stairs with a strange girl. I had achieved a new dimension that bordered on the metaphysical, a sharp delineation of love—not the meaning of the word, but the feeling. I felt like an explorer on the threshold of a strange and wonderful land. I had no idea then that it would be a savage land.

The Second Avenue bus roared into the curb ahead of me. I ran and jumped aboard, swung from an overhead strap until it reached Fourteenth Street, then shouldered my way to the door and the sidewalk.

I walked east passing through the channel of seen-better-days brownstones. It was early, but the street was awake, alive. The East Side is always alive with the harsh, frantic sound of poverty. This is the social cellar of New York and only the language changes. It was Irish once, bawdy and musical with the rolling gaelic vowels; it was Jewish once, hard-pressed dignity and the somber chant of Yiddish; was Italian once, an eruption of sound, a virulent stacatto of language. Now it was Spanish, hopefully musical.

I walked along Fourteenth Street, the social barrier. On the left was the towering maze of the housing project, red brick respectability, angular proper buildings of careful conformity, the sheep pens. And on the right was the east side, the stinking lop-sided spawn of architectural abortion, the fire-escape girded cold water walk-ups, mean low-rent buildings permeated with the rank stomach-turning smell of poverty. Here live die new Americans, the new strong blood, the individualists just waiting for their chance to get across Fourteenth Street and clean conformity.

I turned down on Avenue A and crossed the street to the discolored brick building where I lived. I walked through the brown-walled, trash-littered hallway of the front building, out into the small square courtyard, and stopped. Clotheslines created a colorful design of waving faded underwear. Women were already leaning from the windows, fat bosoms on fat arms, shouting across at other women, comparing the evils of husbands, bemoaning the lost dream.

My building was in the rear, smaller than the front, but more cheerful. Flowering window boxes embraced the windows, classical music blared, five floors of tired, cramped apartments, a tiny center of aspiring artists. Three writers, like myself, two unpublished. A dancer who worked as a waitress. Two actors, one a homosexual, one sculptor, two painters. My place, my friends, all aspiring to success, all living here for one reason—it was cheap.

A sign over the door said: *Dunghill Manor.* My roommate's sense of humor.

I walked into the smell of age and bad plumbing and clorox. Dreams of tomorrow growing in the dunghill of today. I climbed the stairway to the top floor, pushed open the door and I was home.

A kitchen with a large round table and a daybed that served as a couch, a small studio where Claude painted, two cell-like bedrooms.

Claude looked up from his coffee and smiled. "Home from the wars," he said.

I shrugged out of the trench coat. "Scored again," I said. It was the thing to say, but even as I spoke the words I knew that it was too flippant.

"For an old man you do pretty well."

I hung the coat, went to the stove to heat the coffee.

"Who was she?" Claude asked.

"A girl."

"Something new?"

"Different," I said. "Something different."

"Your wife called," he said.

"Oh?" I looked up from the stove. "What did she want?"

"Talk to you."

"She say anything?"

"Wants you to call her. I told her you were at a party with some editor."

I nodded. The coffee was hot. I poured a cup, brought it to the table, pushing my typewriter aside to make room. "Any other happy tidings?"

"Martha called."

"Big night for the phone company."

"I told Martha the same story. She didn't believe it. You were supposed to see her last night."

My past. Part of it. A wife in Connecticut, a girl named Martha. The story of my life—ten years of it. A wife in Connecticut, and always a girl named something. The girls changed in appearance, but that's all. But that was David Markam yesterday. I knew that I had something now, something important, different, real.

"Nice girl, that Martha," Claude said.

"The world's full of them. Nice girls. Too nice."

We talked. We drank coffee. I didn't say anything about Leslie. Generally we would talk about a girl, male talk, comparing her with other girls, talk that would lead into anecdotes of other girls, sometimes funny, sometimes tragic. But I didn't talk about Leslie. I didn't want to compare her, to bring her down to the level of conquest, casual lovemaking. I don't know why. I just couldn't do it. I should have, I suppose. It might have been easier. But hell, there were a lot of things I should have done.

"You think you'll ever get back with your wife?" Claude asked.

I shrugged. "I don't know," I said. "I doubt it. There's nothing there."

"Too bad. I like her."

"So do I. She's a nice girl. But I'm not in love with her." That word again, that damned four-letter word that has no meaning, no definition, and means everything. Love. I must have said it a thousand times. I love you. And every time I said it I knew that it meant nothing. I might have said, I want to touch you, I want to touch a woman. I might have said, I want to lay with you, want to feel the woman-soft of you against me, want the woman-smell in my nostrils, want your voice close to my ear. It was easier to say, I love you.

"Why did you marry her?" Claude asked.

"I don't know. I honest-to-God don't know. I guess I was just ready to get married, and she was there."

"Sounds like a helluva reason to get married."

"Oh, there's more to it than that." It wasn't the kind of thing I wanted to discuss early in the morning, not the kind of thing I wanted to discuss at all, but there was the question, and I had to struggle with the answer. "You can say that you're ready to get married, and that sounds like a reason, but there is always more. With me, I guess I was tired of sleeping around. I knew that I didn't want a lot of women. I wanted a woman I could talk to, someone to share things with. I had one thing and I went to the opposite pole to get something else. I was looking for an intellectual companion. I found her and married her."

"And it wasn't right?"

"No," I said, "not right. The reasons were wrong. The girl was fine, but my motives were wrong. You just don't marry a girl for those reasons. You marry a girl because you want to touch her, because you want to be with her. You marry a girl because she is a woman, because she has warmth. You marry a girl whom you want to lay close to in the dark, not just to make love with, but someone who feels good to hold close to you. I didn't have that. I had someone to talk to, but then I wanted someone soft, someone feminine, someone to understand what I felt, not what I thought."

Claude had a deeply serious look on his face, so I laughed and said, "Ah, screw it, c'mon I've got work to do and my wife problems aren't that interesting."

"She's a nice girl."

"You're right, buddy, and don't think that doesn't make the problem a rough one."

Claude pushed back from the table and stood. "I'm thinking about getting married," he said.

"Think hard about it," I said. "It's not a joke."

"It's very difficult," he said.

"Amen," I said.

He shook his head, then turned and went into the studio. I was alone in the kitchen, alone with thoughts that should not be early morning thoughts. A wife I didn't love; a girl I didn't love; both of them asking me to commit myself to them, and the girl I wanted was almost a stranger.

I got up from the table and took the dishes to the sink. I came back, sat down, pulled the typewriter over, and rummaged through the papers. I checked the writing schedule, saw what I had to produce that day, then leaned back in the chair, rubbing my chin, thinking how nice it might be just to have a job and stop writing garbage.

It was a tough morning. It was getting tougher all the time. In the beginning, when I first began to write for the men's adventure magazines it was a breeze. I was thrilled about being published, I liked the idea of being a professional, and I felt that I could grind out blood and guts without having it affect me. I enjoyed the freedom from the time clock and I got a charge out of concocting the nonsensical plots for the hairy-chested magazines. But lately it had begun to bother me. There was the feeling that I was in a rut, that I was selling myself down the river as a writer. There was the time—a long time ago—when I wanted to be a playwright. But those were hungry days, and I was never sure of my talent. I had hit it as a hack writer. It paid the bills, and I enjoyed it. . . . but lately . . . damn, I knew that it was going to be one of those days.

I stopped for lunch and talked with Claude. It was light talk, mostly about writers and painters, and where we were going to live when we cut the mustard and would have the checks rolling in from the agent. It was dream-talk, wishful thinking in a slum apartment to still the ever-present frustration of failure.

The afternoon was an agony. I tried to work and could not. I smoked until my mouth was raw, drank coffee until the taste of it made me nauseous. I was caught between two machines—the typewriter and the telephone. Perhaps I should have called my wife, or Martha, but I didn't really want to talk to them. The girl. I thought of the girl. I couldn't remember her clearly in the light of day, and there was a dream-like quality about the night before, but I knew she was real, knew that she was there.

I gave up the writing and left the apartment. I walked south along Avenue A, past the one-block concrete excuse for a park. I walked west to First Avenue, drawn by the color and clatter of the street markets, the heady smells of strong spiced meats and cheeses; the European smells of good food and the animated hawking of the merchants. I walked for a long time and when I returned it was growing dark. I stopped for Ravioli at a small place on Second Avenue, then went home for a long evening of pacing the small apartment, and when I could stand it no longer, I walked to 31st Street and stood on the sidewalk in front of her building.

It was a warm night with just the suggestion of a breeze. There was a procession of men and women walking their dogs, typical New York, the lonely cave-dwellers with their lost country youth on a leash.

The windows of her apartment were dark. I crossed the street to the doorway and rang the bell. I waited, but there was no answer.

Strange, but I was elated. It was as though I were compelled to be there, that I had walked the twenty blocks knowing that whatever awaited me, it would not be good, but unable to resist the attraction the girl held for me.

While this may be difficult to accept with credence, one must realize my state of mind at that time. I was completely at odds with myself in matters of love. I honestly believed that it was impossible for me to feel this emotion. There had been many women in my life, and I had felt something for all of them, but it had always paled and each time I knew that I had not touched upon the magical formula of love—whatever it might be. As in any case of frustration the search for love was greatly magnified in my mind until it became inflated beyond importance and was able to overshadow reason. The girl, Leslie, had touched me more deeply than anyone previous, and I had to know what lay beyond the threshold of this emotion called love.

But I was also timid in the possible presence of the unknown, and thus it was a relief to turn and walk away from her doorway.

I walked to Third Avenue and started south, but I stopped before covering a block and turned back. I had to see her. I had to know. I went back to her building and sat on the steps to wait.

The time went slowly. I dislike waiting for any reason. My mind had flights of fancy and I imagined many things, all of them concerned with the girl, all of them bad. I convinced myself that she was a tramp, that she was even then in someone's bed. I decided that she was a hopeless neurotic, a nymphomaniac who picked her men in bars, then got rid of them as quickly as possible. I was mentally castigating myself, successfully soiling my thoughts of her.

I was sullen by the time I saw her come along the street with the man on her arm. Her laughter rippled through the dark, quiet street, and the sound was grotesque to me. I sat unmoving. They reached the steps and stopped, then she saw me. "Oh," she said with surprise. "What are you doing here?"

"Waiting for you," I said.

"Oh." She was at a loss for something to say. I turned my gaze from her to the man at her side. He was middle-aged, somewhat paunchy with a pleasant face that was now furrowed with concern.

"What's up?" he asked.

"Oh," she said, "this . . . this is a friend of mine."

I stood. "I have to see you," I said, ignoring the man at her side.

"I told you not to come back," she said.

"I know. I had to. I had to see you."

"Say, look," the man said, "I don't like to butt in . . ."

"Then don't," I snapped. I came down the steps and stood before her. I stared at her, tried to erase the set lines of anger on her face.

"What is this?" the man said to her.

"Keep out of it," I said. "It doesn't concern you."

"I told you not to come back," she said, and now her voice was tense.

I reached out and took her arm. She wrenched herself free. "Leave me alone," she snapped.

Her companion's voice hardened. "I think that you had better leave," he said.

My anger rose in a flood of frustrating despair. I wanted to speak with the girl and I had not included this third person in my thinking. His interference was annoying. I tried to ignore him. I reached out again and gripped her wrist, holding her tightly. She cried out in pain.

"Just a damn minute, buddy!" Her companion said. He grabbed my arm.

I released her, then turned, dropping into a crouch. I drove a fist into his mid-section. He grunted, surprised, and backed off, doubling over. I raised my hand over my head and chopped down against his neck. He began to go down. I stepped in close and drove my knee into his face, snapping his head back. I chopped him across the throat, then grabbed his lapels, jerking him upright. His face was contorted with surprise and pain. I held him with one hand and drove my fist into his face. He gasped, gagging. I hit him again. I was furious, not at him, at the girl, but I had to strike out at something and he was there. I drove a fist into his stomach and released him. He staggered away, reeling, and clutched a lamppost. He retched, hanging limply, his anguished groans the only sound on the street.

I turned back to the girl, about to speak, but I stopped. She was smiling. It was a strange, gleeful smile. Her forehead glistened with sweat. My voice, when I spoke, seemed to bring her out of a reverie.

"Sorry," I said. "I had to see you."

She recovered and looked at me. Her tongue traced a circular pattern over her lips. She nodded. "Come in," she said.

The man had pushed away from the lamppost and he started up the street, clutching his mid-section and muttering. I watched him go, feeling badly about what I had done. He had done what any man should have done. He hadn't deserved the beating. My conscience was beginning to gnaw, but I shook off the feeling of guilt and followed her through the door.

Inside the narrow vestibule, she stopped and turned to me. "You're strong," she said.

"I know some tricks," I said. "I'm not strong."

She was standing against the wall looking up at me with a mixed expression of awe and pleasure. "He didn't even have a chance to touch you," she said.

"Look," I said, "I'm not proud of that. I was angry. I don't like anger, I don't like fighting. It doesn't prove anything. It never has."

"You won," she said.

"When you win you lose. That's probably a decent guy, I don't know. But because I fight with bastard tactics he lost. But I know how I won, so I lose just a little bit of myself."

She did not answer. She stood there waiting. I leaned forward and placed my hands on her shoulders, holding her lightly. I kissed her, gently placing my lips upon hers, bringing no pressure to bear, treasuring the moment of sensual contact. I moved my lips over her cheek, savoring the perfume smell of her. I pulled her close to me and her arms went about me and we clung together in silence. I felt the soft womanness of her, rejoiced in the way her breasts flattened against me, the pressure of her thighs against mine. I ran my hand along the hollow of her back, listened to her murmur of pleasure. It was a strange feeling at that moment, a feeling of complete relaxation as though I had been searching for something for a long time and had at last come upon it, the kind of feeling you might get after a long, long drive in the desert when you finally reach a destination and know that you can stop.

I released her and stepped back. She continued to look at me for a long moment, then she turned and started up the stairs. I followed. She stopped once and turned and I braced myself for her warning conversation, but she said nothing, turned and continued.

At the top she paused by her door, spoke to the restless dog inside, then opened the door. I followed her as before, along the hallway and into the large room.

I stood by the bar, the big doberman sniffing at me. She went into the bedroom. I leaned over and patted the dog's head. I find something sadistic about keeping dogs in a big city, but what the hell, I could still be nice to the dog.

"Come in here," she said.

I went into the bedroom. She was standing by the closet and pulling her dress over her head. She hung the dress on a hanger, then came across the room in her slip. She passed me, shooed the dog from the room and closed the door. "He's jealous," she said, smiling. She crossed the room to the closet. I sat in a chair and began to light my pipe, watching her.

There was beauty in the way she undressed, a grace that few women possess at such times. I noticed it for the first time that night, but in the months that followed it was to become a ritual that never failed to move me with the natural beauty of her. It was almost like a dance, not the gauche movements of a strip-tease or an exotic, but simpler. The beauty was in the movements of her body and her arms as she removed each piece of clothing.

She turned. "Stop staring," she said.

"I've never seen anything quite so beautiful," I said.

"You make me feel naked."

I smiled and she laughed. "You have a dirty mind," she said, then she moved from the closet and walked, naked, to the bed. She pulled the covers down, slipped beneath the sheets. She sat against the pillows and held the sheet over her breasts. The laughter had left her and her expression was sober. "I wanted to see you again," she said. "I knew that I shouldn't, but I wanted to."

Leaving the chair, I went and sat on the edge of the bed. "I love you," I said. "I want to be close to you."

"But you don't know me!" Her voice was a wail.

"I can only know you by being with you," I said. "I want to know you."

"You don't even know my name."

"Leslie," I said. She looked surprised. "I read it on the mail-box," I said.

She leaned back against the pillows. Her panic was replaced by a smile of intense warmth. "You're too clever for me," she said. "What's your name?"

"David," I said. "David Markam."

"What do you do?"

"I write."

"Under your own name?"

That is never a flattering question for a writer, but I was used to it. "Sometimes," I said.

"What do you write?"

"Magazine stuff. Stories, articles, mostly junk."

"It couldn't be junk," she said.

"Take my word for it," I said. "It's junk."

"But why write junk?"

"It's a living. It beats getting up in the morning, and maybe one day I'll write something good."

"David Markam," she said. "It's a good name. Come to bed, David."

CHAPTER TWO

It was an idyllic week. There was nothing in my life but Leslie, I could think of nothing else, I wanted nothing else. Had it been in my power I would have stopped time, I would have shut us off completely from the rest of the world.

We were together, we found one another, we explored a pathway of love that was new to both of us.

It was a strange newness. It was common-place, something that happens to thousands of men and women in the world every day; they meet, they are attracted to each other, and something grows between them; common-place. And yet, this relationship—just as every relationship—was unique. It was strange and beautiful. A man and a woman are moving through their lives, traveling two distinct paths, and then suddenly they are moving along a single line.

What startled me and delighted me was the uniqueness of the physical relationship. I had known many women, and I had come to expect and accept certain things. While they would all be different, there was also a sameness about them. You could expect certain attitudes from a woman simply because she was a stenographer, or a college graduate, or from the midwest or from a large family. They fell into general moulds in their thinking and only the embellishments made them individuals. This was particularly true in making love. There were patterns, and to me the patterns reduced love-making to boredom. I could be aroused, of course, and I performed the physical act of love with relish, but afterwards it was always a let-down. In a way, it was like buying a glittering object and then finding it tarnished and green and cheap.

It was different with Leslie.

I discovered feelings with her that I would never have believed possible. It was not something I was doing or thinking consciously, and I would not have put it into words if I had not had to make an explanation to Martha.

The meeting was accidental. I was crossing Third Avenue on Fourteenth Street. It was late afternoon, and I was walking east towards my apartment. Martha came out of a drug store just as I stepped onto the curb. We were face-to-face; it was impossible to avoid her. She was as surprised and embarrassed as I.

"Hello, David," she said.

I hesitated a moment. I'm certain that my expression was sheepish—the boy with his hand in the jar of jam. "Hello, Martha," I said, almost with a note of apology.

"I—I haven't seen you," she said.

"I—uh—I've—"

"You've been busy," she said, smiling.

"I don't know quite what to say," I said.

"You don't have to explain yourself to me, David," she said. "You never promised me anything."

It would have been easier if she had been angry. I felt like the original bastard. It was such a damned fool thing. I should have called her, seen her, talked to her; I should have done something, at least. But dammit I hadn't, and now I was facing her. She wasn't just anybody. For christ's sake, two weeks before I had shared her bed, professed a love for her, and now I was wishing that I had been able to avoid her. Damn an understanding woman!

"Are you in a hurry?" I asked.

"You want to get rid of me already?"

"No," I said, embarrassed. "I just thought we might get a cup of coffee."

"I'd love it," she said.

"There's an expresso place on Seventeenth."

"Fine."

We walked to the curb and had to wait for the light. It was a tense and annoying moment. It might have been easier if we could have kept moving, but the pause brought up the necessity for conversation. I wasn't in the right frame of mind to make street conversation. I had dumped this girl without even a phone call, and whether she was going to be big about it or not, I just couldn't get over the feeling of guilt.

"How have you been?" I asked.

"You don't have to make polite talk, David," she said.

I bit on my lip. I was on the verge of anger. Was she trying to make a fool of me? No, I had done that myself. I broke into a smile, and it spread to a guilty grin. "You're a mind reader," I said.

The light changed. "I think I know a little about you," she said. We crossed the street.

Walking along we said nothing. The routine of walking with her had a disturbing influence upon me. It was so natural. I must have covered half the damned city at her side, walking and talking. What had we talked about? God knows. Just about everything, I suppose. Writing, a lot about writing. Usually, *but, David, it seems like such a waste for you to be writing the type of things you do. You have so much more to offer.* And me saying, *I have to eat. I've got a wife and kids to feed.* And her answer, *you could get a job.* And me saying. *I'm a writer, dammit, that's my job. I do the job. It's crap, but so are most jobs.* And she says, *It's not just a job and you know it. You can write, David, and it's a shame to waste it.* And then I would be annoyed and angry because I agreed with everything she said, but was too damned afraid to really try to write something decent, and then I would bring up the kids again as the buffer against my own frustration, *Look, I'm a hack writer with kids to feed. Let somebody else write the pretty prose. I know my limitations. I'm a hack and I'm proud of it.* But always afterwards, when I would be alone at the typewriter, the dream would grow out of her chiding, and I would find myself writing harder, looking for the elusive phrase to make the story better, stronger, more concise. And on those walks we covered other subjects: Marriage, love, parenthood, art, politics—name a subject and we worried it in agreement or argument. Yes, I guess Martha did know a little about me.

"Penny for your thoughts," she said.

"What? . . . oh . . ." I laughed, caught unaware. "You're the mind reader," I said.

"Sometimes I wish I were," she said.

"Do you, Marthe? Would you really like to always know what people are thinking?"

"No, I guess not," she said, frowning. "I'd hate it, really. There are too many times that you want to fool yourself into believing that they're thinking something else. There are times when you want to be beautiful and you make yourself feel beautiful. It would be terrible to know that you weren't."

I started to answer, then checked myself. Damn! It was too easy to fall into this. Martha was the kind of girl you talked to. She was a pretty girl with a full, shapely body, and you could be initially attracted to her physically, but within an hour, she became a girl to talk to. I remember her saying once: *I'm the sister type, every mans sister, and just once, just one time I'm going to be someone's woman.* Even with me. It was a week before I kissed her, and even though I could sense the longing in her, a latent power of unexplored womanness, I pulled back, wary of her. I often tried to say that I was being decent, that she was too nice to be hurt, but it was an excuse. With Martha it would be important and a man would have to be one hell of a lot of man to match her womanness. And I was unsure of myself. So we talked, and it was comfortable and good. I liked her and in time this grew into a kind of comfortable love. I don't know what it was. It seemed good at the time. There were no problems with her, and when we slept together, made love, it was as though we had been married for years. It might have gone on if I hadn't met Leslie.

We reached the coffee house and took a table in the rear. It was quiet. Classical music formed a soft background and the light was dim. We sat, looking, uncomfortable, trying to find the level of conversation.

"Is she nice, David?"

I didn't answer immediately. It was the kind of thing she would say. I wasn't surprised. "I don't know," I said, finally.

We were silent again. The waiter came and went. I was wishing that I were somewhere else. I didn't really want to talk about Leslie, but now that it had been brought up, there didn't seem to be anything else that I could do.

"I figured that there was someone else," Martha said. "I called a few times and Claude was too evasive."

"He likes you," I said.

"Yes."

The waiter brought the coffee and now there was something to do. A spoon to fool with, coffee to stir, a place for the eyes that did not want to meet hers.

"You want to talk about it, David?"

"I'm not sure," I said.

"It's none of my business, really," she said. "It's just that . . . that . . . well, I guess I'm basically . . ."

"Marthe," I reached across the table and covered her hand with mine. She looked down and bit her lip. "Marthe, I don't know quite what to say. I feel a little rotten about . . . well, about things. Seeing you, I realize how shabby I've been."

"You're not," she said. She smiled, but her eyes were misted. "You could never be anything like that, David. If you did anything wrong it was only because you couldn't bear to hurt anyone."

"But I hurt you more."

"You didn't mean to," she said. "I'll admit, David, that I was hurt that you wouldn't talk to me, but I know that it was only because you were afraid of the tears and recriminations. You're a very nice man, David Markam."

"You're making me feel worse," I said.

"Of course," she said, smiling, "that's what I'm trying to do."

We laughed together, then I sobered. "Marthe, you know . . ."

"If you tell me I'm a nice girl I'll scream," she said. "I don't want to be a nice girl!"

We were silent again, thoughtfully quiet for what seemed a long time, then Martha asked, "David, what is she like?"

"What do you mean?"

"I mean what is there about her, whoever she is, that I don't have? I'm a girl, I know I'm attractive, I have warmth. I was good in bed with you. Why couldn't I hold you?"

"It's hard to explain. I know that it's not a matter of holding someone. It's . . . well . . . dammit, Marthe, I don't know."

"Chemistry?"

"The time-worn explanation," I said. "But it's something like that. I met her in a bar and three hours later I was in bed with her. It's the sort of thing you'd expect from a tramp, but that's not it. I'm in love with her, Martha, that's all I can say. I never knew what it was like to be in love before. I mean, I thought I was in love, but now I know that I wasn't. This girl throws everything else into focus. I'm not sure just what it is with her, but being with her makes me realize that everything before her fell short of the mark."

"She's a lucky woman," Marthe said

"Maybe."

"Did you . . . did you ever feel anything for me?"

"I felt a lot. I felt an awful lot. But, Marthe, with this girl it just isn't like anything else. If I could just explain it. It's . . . it's like . . . oh, damn, I don't know. It sounds foolish in words. Sometimes I'm standing in a room and she is there, maybe reading a book, and she looks up, and I hold her eyes for a moment, and I'm suddenly filled with this feeling of great elation, as though I own the whole damned world."

"Are you going to marry her?"

"Marry?"

"I mean, if you love someone . . . well . . . I suppose you want to marry them."

I stared into my coffee, perplexed. Marriage. It had never occurred to me. Why not? Why had I never thought of Leslie in terms of wife? "I don't know," I said.

"It's something you don't like to face, isn't it?"

"Wouldn't say that. It's . . . it's just that . . . well, it hasn't come up."

"She doesn't want to get married?"

"I don't know."

"Would you marry her?"

The conversation was running along the wrong tack. I scowled, not liking it. Martha had a way of driving into the core of a thing, peeling away protective coverings to expose nerves to the air. She forced you to look into yourself, to examine the motives behind your actions, and this is seldom pleasant. What she was really saying was: *Are you sure about this, or are you creating a romantic image of what you want a woman to mean to you? Are you willing to place this woman on a scale balanced against your two children, or are you afraid to face the ultimate decision of this choice?*

"It's something I'll have to face when the time comes," I said.

"You're evading it, aren't you?"

"No. I've known this girl for a week. She's like nothing I have ever known. It's important, but I don't believe that you have to have marriage to sustain love. I've been married; I am married, and it has nothing to do with love."

"You love your children."

"Yes, and I'm not married to them."

She smiled. "You win," she said. "Oh, David, please don't think I'm trying to belittle what you feel. Believe me, it's a wonderful thing. I'd give anything to have you feel that way about me. It's just that I . . ." She paused, a slight catch to her voice. She glanced down at her folded hands, then looked up. "Oh, David, I just want you to have what is right. You have so much to give, so much feeling, and I hate to think of anyone soiling it." She stopped abruptly, swallowed and closed her eyes. She opened her eyes and smiled. "I'm sorry," she said.

"Marthe," I said, caught up in the absolute honesty of the girl. "Marthe, if I . . . I . . . oh, hell, there's nothing to say."

"I know what you mean, David. I'm a good friend."

"No, it's not that. You're more than that. You're . . . oh, dammit, Marthe, I feel so goddamned ineffectual. I want to say things to you, want to reach out and touch you with words, and I don't have them."

"David," she said, spacing her words carefully, looking closely into me, "I love you. I'm not a martyr, but I do know that there are times when you love someone you can only express that love by sending them away from you. The love I feel for you will be stronger in knowing that you have something you want, knowing that you have a contentment. For a time I filled a gap in your life. You were sincere, I know that. We made some plans, looked ahead when we should not have, but that doesn't matter. A relationship must always look ahead, it's the way people are, but it doesn't mean that it is anyone's fault if the future ends with the present. It had to end sometime, and no matter when it ended it would have been the present and there would still be a future unfulfilled. I loved you, David, and you brought a great deal into my life, and out of it all I have only one regret." She paused, waiting for me to say something. I kept quiet. "Do you know what I regret?"

"What?"

"The weekend we were always going to spend together. We never did it. I would have liked to have had that weekend."

There was nothing I could say. Damn! How does a man get so fouled up with people? It never starts off that way, but it grows and grows, and then you're up to your clavicle in problems. Why can't it remain simple and uncomplicated. Every year of your life you get deeper and deeper in people until there comes a time when you feel swamped, and out of the maze of people you find yourself struggling to find yourself, trying to establish the identity that is your own, and with each pull away from the peopled past you only sink into the morass of more people. If only you didn't have an effect on others it might be easier, but a man walks hand-in-hand with the world and whenever he goes off the path he has to pull; someone else out of line. There are times when you wish that you were just a damned vegetable.

I was angry with myself and angry with Marthe for the contrast she presented against my self-indulgent son of a bitch attitude of being concerned with number one.

"We'd better go," she said.

"Yeah."

We left the coffee house and walked back to Fourteenth Street. We said nothing. It was all said. It was over, so what can you say? *Happy Days? Good Show? Nice to have known you?* It would all sound like so much crap. Better to say nothing.

We parted at the comer. She held out her hand and I pressed it. Thank God, there were no brave smiles; Just, "Goodbye, David," and she turned and walked south. I stood for a moment watching her, then I crossed the street and headed for Avenue A.

I was on my way home. I had spent the afternoon uptown talking to editors. I had several assignments for stories and I was going to work. But my mind was filled with Martha and Leslie. I stopped at the corner of First Avenue. I had to see her. I had to see her against the background of Martha, see her in the new light of having tried to put her into words.

And I found another side to Leslie.

The First Avenue bus let me off at her street and I walked west to the apartment house and pushed through the door after her answering buzz. I climbed the stairs, reached the top breathing hard, and lifted my hand to knock. The door opened. Leslie stood there.

"Hello," I said.

Without a word she flung herself across the threshold. My arms came up automatically and she fell against me, clinging, burrowing her face into my chest. Behind her, in the hallway, the dog whimpered.

I was stunned. I held her close and her body trembled under my hands. Her shoulders shook and her crying was muffled. I stroked her hair. "Leslie," I said, "Leslie, what's wrong?"

"Don't leave me, David," she said. "Please, don't leave me."

"But I'm here," I said. "I'm not going to leave you."

"David, I'm afraid." She lifted her face and deep within the pupils of her eyes I could see the terror there, an unmasked horror that obviously lurked in her mind, an inconsolable loneliness. "Don't leave me, David. I don't know what I'd do without you now, David. Please, please say you won't leave me."

"I have no intention of leaving you, Leslie." I turned her back into the apartment, closed the door, and led her along the hallway. She stopped suddenly, turning and shoving against me so that I was backed against the wall. "David," she wailed, "I'm frightened!"

I gripped her shoulders hard. I did not know what to say. The outburst was confusing and erratic and I wanted to shake her and tell her to get hold of herself, that I had no intention of leaving her, and that she was imagining things. I said nothing. I held her close, actually welcoming and enjoying the Strength she thrust upon me, feeling my importance to this girl's wellbeing.

In time she became quiet. She sighed deeply and straightened. She shook her head, fluffed the blonde hair, then suddenly she gave a short laugh.

"David," she said gaily, as if nothing had been said, "how nice to see you." She took my hand in hers and preceded me along the hallway and into the large living room.

I was scowling, wondering what in hell's name the hysterical scene had been about, getting just a bit angry. I had the feeling that the whole bit had been an act, some sort of weird joke that she had put on as a whim. I didn't like it.

Leslie went behind the bar. "Drink?" she asked.

"Scotch," I said, still trying to contain the anger that was gradually building.

"Have a martini with me," she said.

"All right."

I turned and walked the length of the room. I stood by the window looking north to the Empire State Building. I watched the searchlight sweep over Manhattan. The dog came and nuzzled at my leg. I dropped my hand and scratched its head.

It was disturbing, this feeling that the scene had not been a whim at all, but genuine hysteria suddenly forgotten.

"Drinks are on," Leslie said.

I went back to the bar. We drank several martinis and talked. It went on for several hours, then I remembered the work awaiting me at home, and said that I had to leave.

A flash of panic appeared in her eyes. The conversation faltered. She attempted to ignore the fact that I had to go home, then said, "Get something on the radio, will you, David."

I nodded and slid off the bar stool. The radio was on the dresser in the bedroom. I was there working the dial when she came in, passed by me and went to the closet. She was hurrying and I watched her. She began to undress, slipping the sweater over her head, unzipping the tight slacks and pulling them off her legs. It was all too obvious. She had no intention of having me leave and was about to offer what she knew would keep me there. It was too planned, too exacting. It was the first weakness in our relationship. It was too desperate. It gave me a feeling that is impossible to explain, a kind of foreboding.

"David?"

I had turned to the radio, but I was aware of her movements as she pulled back the covers and climbed into the bed. I turned at her bidding.

She was smiling. I was annoyed, not so much at her as with myself. I had the feeling that there was a flaw in my character, a weak spot, and that she knew about it and could play upon it. But despite the annoyance I was struck by her beauty; the blonde hair, golden under the warmth of the bed lamp, spread on the pillow; the nakedness of her shoulders, and the slight swell of the beginning of her breasts.

"Come here, David."

I went to the bed and sat on the side away from her. She pouted and patted the bed at her side. "Over here, David, I want you to be close to me for just a moment before you leave."

There was no point in showing reluctance. I wanted to be close to her. I knew that I should not move, that I should have left then, but I wanted to be close to her. I got up and circled the bed. She held up her arms. I sat down, then leaned into the enclosure of her arms and buried myself and my doubts and my thoughts in the woman scent of her.

"Stay with me, David," she whispered, "please stay with me."

I did not answer. It was not necessary. I wanted to stay within the mind-consuming warmth of her. I knew that I would. It was inevitable.

But as I held her to me in the later darkness of the room, our bodies sated of desire, but clinging, feeling her breath upon my neck, feeling the press of her from neck to thigh, I was frightened; frightened for myself, because I knew that I was lost.

CHAPTER THREE

I t was the end of the month and I was making the duty call to wife and children. It shouldn't be called that, I suppose, but that is what it generally amounted to.

The idea that a man can be a parent two days a month is pure nonsense. Becoming a father is one thing. You're a father biologically and you remain so through your life. No matter what happens, you are still the father of the children you conceive. It is a meaningless thing. Being a parent is quite another activity. This takes time and effort, and is something that one does by choice. You don't make it as a parent on two days a month.

These monthly trips never failed to increase my bitterness towards the situation with Marion. The kids were great and I honestly loved them both. I just couldn't take their mother. So, I always came out of these trips the complete bastard. Why? Because I could not stand to be in the same room with that damned female—as simple as that.

The train swayed and labored through the Connecticut countryside; postcard pretty on both sides, the rolling hills, the neat farm clusters, the stone fences that always made me think of the Revolutionary War and Minute-Men crouched with blunderbuss waiting for the Red Coats. It was Saturday, a warm, sunny day. The car of the train was filled; it was stuffy; I wished that I had rented a car.

I sat by the window, bored, counting telegraph poles as they swept past, glancing at disinterested cows and horses; I tried to place myself back in the suburban life, compared it to the way I was now living, found the whole thing unreal and depressing. I had the usual trappings of the visiting father; the flowers for Marion, the two books and two toys for the children; the bric-a-brac of a man's guilt, the payoff.

Where is it that a man's life gets screwed up? I could remember back to childhood and it all seemed so simple. There was high school and the biggest problem was how to get the family car for the week-end. The real problems, the kind that were like ice in the guts, started and ended with sex. There was that girl, Clara, the hot number in town. I went for a walk with her one summer night, walking and talking, and nervous, knowing what I was after, knowing that Clara knew what I was after, being led by her to a special place she knew about. I was scared, but excited. This was it. This was what the guys talked and laughed about. I was frightened because I had given Clara a lot of big talk, and I had not the remotest idea of what I was sup- posed to do. I could have saved myself the worry. Clara knew where she was going and what she was going to do, and she was a patient teacher. I'll admit that it was quite a letdown, but then I had a full month of feeling certain that the girl was pregnant. It was plenty to worry about, but it didn't stop me from taking other walks with Clara.

Finally you get married. Why? What is there about one girl that makes you marry her? In my case I say that it was boredom. I was simply tired of sleeping around and wanted to settle down to the full, complete relationship with one woman. And when I had that feeling I happened to be going with Marion. Maybe it was more than that. I don't really know, but I do know that the moment I turned from the minister and faced Marion, seeing her as my wife, I knew that it was a mistake.

The conductor came down the aisle announcing East Trumble. I watched the train roll into the run-down cluttered outskirts of the town, and when I knew that we were near the station, I got up from the seat and went to the door.

I took a cab at the station. In another age, another life, Marion used to meet me. The smiling, suburban wife, the peck on the cheek, the drive home—a complete bore.

There was the street. The neat, identical houses; the neat, identical patches of lawn; the neat, identical cars in the neat, identical driveways; the neat, identical wives; the neat, identical children. East Trumble. Home is where the heart is. The cab stopped, I paid the fare, got out and walked into the squeals of two children eager to get their gifts.

The week-end, as expected, was a disaster.

I went through the motions of parenthood. The children reacted to the routine visit with the exuberance of a holiday, and the old feelings of responsibility assailed me.

To whom or what does a man owe his life? Should he be true to himself or should he live a lie? Does he owe his life to a marriage? These are questions I had asked myself a thousand times and there were no simple answers. I had two children. They were young, just beginning their struggle with life. They were the innocent victims of a broken home. Did I owe these two children my life? Would it make a difference to them whether or not I lived with them? Questions, Questions, the damnable unanswerable questions that beat against the mind with the numbing persistance of a metronome.

The children wandered off to play and I was alone in the house with Marion. We were in the living room, amidst the usual time-payment furnishings, the trappings of the stifling suburban conformity. I sat on the divan and Marion stood by the fireplace that was never lighted.

"Care for a drink?" she asked.

"Have scotch?"

"I think there's a little," she said. "On the rocks?"

"Fine."

She left the room to fix the drink. I leaned back and looked about me. There was my chair. *My chair.* There had been a big production about making certain that I had my own chair, the unassailable throne, the symbol of the head-of-the-house. That was a long time ago. I was a stranger here, now. I was still making the payments on the house, but it had nothing to do with me. But then, it had always been Marion's house. The chair, that cubicle had been reserved for me.

Marion returned with the drink. She sat on the chair across from me.

"How have you been?" she asked.

"So-so," I said.

"How is the city?"

"Warm, crowded. You know, 'the usual rat-race."

"Yes."

The conversation died. I twirled the ice cubes in the glass. Marion went to the record player. Background music to relieve the tension.

"I saw Dick Berger," Marion said.

"Oh?"

"He was a bit concerned about you."

Berger was a magazine editor and he had rejected my last two stories. The hell with him, I thought. Like all editors, a frustrated no-talent writer. They had to reject just to assert themselves. He lived in East Trumble.

"Nice of him," I said.

Marion ignored my sarcasm. "He seems to think that you might have written yourself out."

"What would he know about writing?"

Marion shrugged. "He was genuinely concerned," she said. "He seemed to think that maybe something was bothering you."

"Look, Marion," I said, keeping my voice low and steady, "I don't give a particular damn what Dick Berger thinks."

She was silent a moment, then she said. "You have the same old reaction to criticism."

"Meddling, not criticism." There was an edge to my voice now. Damn! I didn't want to get into a hassle with her.

"Are you eating right, getting enough sleep?"

"Oh, for christ sake, Marion, get off it." I was annoyed now. Marion sincerely believed that the ills of the world could be cured with enough wheat germ and vitamins. There is nothing more irritating than having an estranged wife firmly believe that a balanced diet could save a marriage.

"Well, you don't take care of yourself."

"Don't worry about it, Marion. I won't fall apart and not make it to the typewriter. I'll get the money in, don't worry." It was an unfair thing to say, but it had the usual effect.

"I'm not concerned about that," she snapped.

I closed my eyes and spread my hands. "Okay, okay. Let's just forget it."

"I still happen to be your wife," she said.

"Let's forget it, Marion."

"It's easy for you to forget it," she said, the edge of hysteria growing in her voice. "You have your little nest in the city and your entourage of females."

"Let's forget it."

"No, I won't forget it. David, those children out there are yours. When are you going to grow up and accept your responsibilities?"

I got up from the divan and went to the window. I was already thinking about the train back to New York, eager to get away. Escape? Yes, but what; what was I escaping? Was Marion right? Was I really running from responsibility? I accepted economic responsibility with ease. I might live in near poverty myself, but Marion and the kids had all that they needed. But I knew that I could not face the emotional responsibility for wife and kids, and this bothered me.

"Marion," I said, "it won't work. Let's not fight about it. I've tried and it won't work."

"You never give it a chance."

I felt suddenly weary. "I have tried," I said. "I have tried more than you know." I turned from the window and walked to the center of the room. She was waiting for me to speak, and I would try to explain it again, even though I knew that it would have no effect upon her. "Marion," I said, "I'm truly sorry about this situation, believe me. You feel that I'm juvenile in my thinking. You may be right, but that still does not stop me from feeling the way I do about things, and I have to live with die way I feel. It is important to me that I feel love for the woman I live with. You don't seem to realize that my life would be a simpler thing if I could live here with you. But I can't. I'm not in love with you."

"Your grade school idea of love."

"Let me finish."

"I don't see what you—"

"Please, Marion."

She was silent, but there was a grim determination about her that I knew would refuse to accept the truth of anything I might say. It was hopeless, but I felt that it had to be said; for myself as much as for her. "Love to me is a lot of things, but one of the basic necessities is an unspoken tenderness between two people."

"You've been reading your stories again."

"Dammit, Marion, shut up and listen!" I paused, waiting for my irritation to subside, then I went on. "This love thing I have to have is wanting to reach out and touch the person. I suppose that seems too simple, but it is a basic truth. Just to suddenly want to cover her hand with mine."

"I think I hear violins."

I stopped after her sarcastic interruption. "Okay," I said, "just forget it."

"That doesn't solve anything," she said.

"It can't be solved the way you want it," I said. "Marion, for God's sake, get it through your head that I cannot live with you."

"Because you have to have some slut!" she snapped. "Oh, brother, don't think that I don't know what the real problem is. You just have to have those cheap tramps around you!"

What was the use of talking. There was a wall between us that could not be penetrated. Marion was a wife first and a woman second. She saw everything from the peculiar attitude of American Wife. To her a girl like Martha would always be a tramp; a girl like Leslie would be even worse. It has to do with fear, I know, but more than that it is the product of the mythology of husband and wife. The American girl is trained from childhood in the art of securing a husband. This is her insurance, her personal retirement plan. She supports the cosmetics industry in this quest, spends hours dancing or talking or indulging in sports activity to give the appearance of the perfect mate. But when she succeeds, she feels that she can at last relax, that the battle has been won. Even when she suddenly realizes that her mate is disenchanted, that the marriage is drifting, her thinking is dictated by what she feels are the inalienable rights of the wife. She got her husband, her meal-ticket; let other women get their own the same way she did, just so long as they stay out of her territory. The fact that this attitude collides head-on with the basics of human nature mean nothing to her; she wears emotional blinders. What is hers is hers, and that's all that there is to it.

"Well," she said, "who is she this time?"

"Let's just forget it."

Forget it, forget it. Is that all you can say?"

"Marion, I don't want to fight about this."

"I have a right—"

"You have no rights over me!" I was angry then, and I went on with a rush of words. "You lost any rights to me when I left your bed! You won't realize it or accept it, but that's where a marriage is made."

"You've got a—"

"Dirty mind! Yes, that's what I've got! I believe that the relationship between a man and woman must be largely physical or it can't exist. I don't only think that sex is important, I think it's a damned absolute essential! When a man first looks at a woman it is physical; when he touches her it's physical. A man wants his wife to be wanted by him, goddamit, and if that's having a dirty mind then I've got it! Everytime I ever touched you I felt that you were giving up that jewel more precious than life itself!"

"Don't be funny!"

"It's not funny, Marion, it's damned well not funny!"

There, at last, was the problem, and I suppose it was mine. Marion was quite willing to carry on a polite separate-bedroom marriage and I could not. Sex. The world revolves and evolves on it. Show me a problem, a frustration, and at the bottom of it all will be sex. There was nothing more to say.

CHAPTER FOUR

The days piled one upon the other; the city became warmer and warmer as if the concrete held back a portion of each days heat and added it to the next day.

It had been a particularly hot day, but the sun had gone down and now a thin breeze was stirring. It was the kind of day that people rush from air-conditioning to air-conditioning, the dull shock showing on their faces during the interim.

I was in the Mansfield Bar on 44th St., drinking beer and listening to my agent.

"You've got to make up your mind, Dave," he said. "You're either a writer or a lover."

"C'mon, Sam, it's not that bad."

He narrowed his eyes. He ran a hand over his balding head, then brought the hand down and pointed one finger. "Dave," he said, seriously, "I'm not kidding. I've met this girl, and I say that she's bad news."

"It has nothing to do with her. I'm in a bit of slump. It happens to all writers."

"Call it what you want. Say you've got writer's cramp. I happen to know different. It's that broad."

"What have you got against her?"

"I got against her that she's hurting one of my writers, that's what. Dave, I know you. I been handling you from the start. You can't do anything half-way. You're impetuous, you throw yourself into things. This has been good for your work, but it's minder when you tangle with a broad."

JUDGE NOT MY SINS

"There have been other women."

"Yeah, but you always dumped them when they got into your hair. This broad is a kook, Dave, and she's gonna have you on your butt."

"You're wrong, Sam. If anything, she always wants to help me with my work."

"I'll bet," he said, "and I know just what kind of help. She want you to be a better writer, to stop the commercial stuff and write something great. That's right, isn't it? Agh, don't answer. I know these broads. Kid, that kook will have you so far out in left field on the Great American Novel that it will take ten years to get back."

"What have you got against quality?"

"Ah!," he snorted. "Ah . . . ah-ha! I hit it didn't I. So she wants you to write quality." He grimaced, shaking his head. "Kid, for christs sake, will you get it through your head that you write quality. You write blood and guts, but you're better than average because you always put more into it. You're growing, and each day you get better, but, boy, keep your head. There are a lot of steps on this ladder. You're climbing them one at a time, and each time you take a step you're sure of yourself because you've got damned good footing on the rung under you. You suddenly take a leap at the top and you're gonna fall on your ass."

"You think I'm not good enough."

"Agh, for christs sake, cut out the temperament. You're not talking to some art nut. I'm your agent. I own ten percent of your future."

"Ten percent of nothing."

"Stop looking for sympathy. David, boy, you've got talent. I know it and you know it, but your talent is a special kind. One guy comes along and writes a book, and wham, it's a hit. He happens to have been ready to write a book. You're a different kind of writer. You have to grow by writing, and that's what you're doing. You started out on newspapers, then moved into pulp fiction and articles, and now you're moving into a little better market. In a

3 5

while you'll do some paperback books, and in time you'll move up to better things. In the meantime you keep meeting the challenge of what you're doing."

"That has nothing to do with the present problem," I said.

"Right. The present problem is that dame."

"The present problem is the fact that I can't seem to write this garbage anymore."

"Crap! It's tlie broad!"

"Lay off her, Sam!"

No, dammit. Besides being your agent I'm also your friend. I'm going to tell you something and you're going to listen, because I'm the boy who has to go to bat when you foul up on an assignment, and you happen to have missed five assignments this month, and I've got five angry editors." He took a deep breath, and I kept silent. "I'm going to tell you something about that girl. She may be a sweet looking thing, but she's a witch. That's a girl who likes trouble, and another thing she likes is to castrate a man. You say, she wants to help you; I say she wants to ruin you. If you can't write, and that happens to be the one thing you do well, then she has complete control over you. Take my word for it, Dave, that girl wants you to fall on your face."

"Sam, I'm happy with this girl."

"Happy! What the hell does happy have to do with it? I'd rather have you miserable and working. For christs sake, if the world was happy the damned place would fold up in a week!"

"You'd rather have me back with Marion."

"Right! That's exactly where I would like to see you. At least you got some work done, and the writing was good."

"I know that, and I know why. I stayed in my work room because I'd rather be there behind the typewriter than in the room with her. I was driven to that damned machine out of a frustration, and I wrote in anger."

"Good! Thank God for miserable marriages, or nothing would get written!"

"I couldn't go back to that, Sam," I said. "I'd rather give up writing."

He was silent, then. He knew that I meant it. He wrinkled his round, homely face, and shook his head. I knew that he was genuinely concerned about me, but I also knew that he could never understand the way I felt about things.

"Life gets fouled up sometimes, don't it?" he said.

I smiled. "Amen," I said.

"Look, kid, I don't want to make you sore at me, but take my advice and get rid of that girl."

"I can't."

He took a deep breath and sighed. "Do you realize how much money you kicked this last month? Seven hundred and fifty dollars. That ain't peanuts. If Marion don't get her check there's going to be hell to pay."

"I'm thinking about it."

"You better do more than think about it."

"I've been thinking of getting a job."

"Is that gonna help your writing?"

Sam was too right and I didn't like it. The money monster was perched on my shoulders. I glanced at my watch. "I better be rolling," I said.

"Get rid of her, Dave."

I got up from the table. "Yeah. Well, thanks for the drink."

"That story for Berger is due tomorrow," he said.

"I'll have it done," I said. "I'll work tonight."

"See you in the morning," he said.

I said goodnight to Andy, the night bartender at the Mansfield, and pushed out into the heat. It was like walking under a heavy blanket.

I hailed a cab, settled back against the leather seat, and gave Leslie's address. The cab crawled down Fifth Avenue, then across to Third, and down. I got out at 31st and walked east.

She was standing in the open doorway, the dog at her side, when I labored to the top of the stairs.

The radiance of her welcoming smile nullified anything that Sam might have said against her. It was ridiculous to imagine that Leslie could be anything but good for me. She made me feel that it was important that I be there, that I was an integral part of her existence. I had never known a girl before who did not bore me after a time, who did not become a drag as she stupidly wheedled her way into my life. With Leslie it was always as though I were meeting her for the first time. There was always the intrigue, the mystery, the vicarious pleasure that you get from the chance meeting; everything is new and challenging, an uncharted sea.

"Hi," she said in the soft melodic tone that always said so much more than the simple word. "How did it go?"

"Terrible," I said. "The editorial world doesn't like me."

"They don't know you," she said. "Come, let me get you a drink."

She clutched my arm and leaned against me as we went along the hallway to the living room, then she broke away and went behind the bar. She made martinis, maintaining a running commentary about nothing as she went through the motions. I have always hated small-talk, but coming from Leslie, it was pleasant.

The apartment was comfortably air conditioned and it was a welcome relief from the street, and I was thinking ahead to my own stuffy, hot apartment.

We sipped the drinks against a background of a Franck symphony.

"Let's go to a movie tonight," she said.

I was slightly startled. We had never been to a film before. As a matter of fact, we seldom went out. I hadn't thought about it before, but our entire social life consisted of meeting occasionally at the Mansfield or a small party with friends of mine. It occurred to me then that I had never met any friends of Leslie's. As far as I was concerned she had no past. There were many telephone calls, and it was evident by what she said that most of the calls were from men, but there was never any mention of anyone, and we never met anyone she knew. It was strange, but I had never thought of it before. And now, suddenly, she wanted to go to a movie.

"I can't tonight," I said. "I've got work to do."

"Ohhh," she said, disappointed.

"I'm sorry," I said, "but this is important. It's a firm assignment and I need the money bad."

"I think I hate those editors," she said. "You ought to be working on a novel anyway."

"That's a nice thought, but novels pay very little money. And right now I need money or I'm going to have two starving children."

"Ah, well," she said, cheerfully, "another time."

That was the end of it, and we talked about other things. It grew dark, and I checked my watch.

"I've got to go," I said. "Duty calls."

"Work here," she said.

"No, I think I'd better go home. I have to get this thing completed by tomorrow, and I'll be working all night."

"I promise not to bother you," she said.

I was skeptical and it was obvious. "I don't think so," I said. "I don't think that I could stay away from you all night."

"I'll lock my door," she said. "It will just be nice to have you in the house. You can work in the office. Everything is there. Paper, carbon, everything."

"Well ... I ... uh ..."

"Oh, c'mon. I promise. I won't bother you, and if you leave the typewriter I'll send you right back. If you go home you'll just die of the heat."

She had a point and a good one. I dreaded the thought of the hot apartment awaiting me. It was under the roof and would be like an oven.

"Okay," I said, "but seriously, I really must get this damn thing written."

She was childishly delighted, as though I was doing her some great favor by agreeing to work in her apartment. I could only think that Sam could not have been more wrong, that if anything would get me out of my writing slump, it would be Leslie's enthusiasm.

I followed her into the office. She rushed about turning on lights, clearing away the clutter on the desk, swinging the typewriter into position, getting paper from the desk. Her production was making me feel foolish.

"That's fine," I said, "that will be just fine."

"Try the chair."

I sat down. She fussed about. "Is it comfortable?" I nodded that it was. "You're sure? I can get another chair."

"It's fine," I said.

She stood back and looked over the scene; me sitting at the typewriter, ready to go to work. She tilted her head, smiling, as though she was gazing at a flower arrangement of her own handiwork.

"How do I look?" I said.

"Like a writer," she said.

"Then let me write."

She bowed, still smiling, then left the room. I filled my pipe and lit it. I leaned back in the chair, stared at the blank paper. I knew the story that I had to write. Hell, I had already written the same damned story fifty times. All I had to do was change the characters. But a story, even the same tired plot, has got to start somewhere. I sat for a few minutes, then I began.

It went slowly, but I kept at it steadily for several hours. Leslie brought me coffee, favored me with a kiss on the forehead and left the room. I had the feeling that she was playing a game; a charade in which she was cast as the typical helpmate to the struggling artist.

By midnight it was obvious that I was right, and that she was now tired of the game. She came into the office.

"Aren't you finished yet?" she asked.

I looked up from the typewriter. "I'll be here all night," I said. "It goes slowly."

"Why don't you let it go until tomorrow?"

"Because it has to be turned in by tomorrow," I said.

She scowled, turned and left the room. I went back to work, but then she returned. "Why don't you take a break," she said. "I don't have anyone to talk to."

"Leslie," I said wearily, "I have to get this thing finished. I told you when I agreed to work here that it would take all night."

"I know that, but I'm bored."

"You promised not to bother me."

She walked the length of the room and looked through the window, then she turned and paced the room. The dog came into the room and joined her in her pacing.

"Look," I said, "I'm trying to work. Would you mind going into the other room?"

"I'd mind," she said.

"But I can't work with you walking around in here."

She stopped and scowled and was about to say something, then she changed her mind. She left the room with the dog at her heels.

I heard the television suddenly turned on, and a few minutes later it went off. The radio came on next. I heard her humming, then she appeared in the doorway. "I want you to come to bed," she said.

"I can't. I have to work." The irritation was honing the edge of my words.

"Work! All you want to do is work!"

"Leslie, for christs sake, I've got to get this done."

"Well, I want you to come to bed."

I ignored her and concentrated on the page in the typewriter. She came into the room and stood in front of me. "Are you coming to bed?"

"No."

The expression on her face then was—how can I explain it?—it was mischievous and malicious. It was as though she had accepted a challenge and was delighted with the prospect of combat. She smiled just slightly and there was a smouldering insolence in her eyes. Perhaps the maliciousness was in my own mind, I don't know, but I was angry with her, because I knew at that moment, whatever it was she had in mind—I was going to lose.

She stood before me, just beyond the circle of light from the overhead lamp. She was wearing a white cotton blouse and skirt. Without taking her eyes from me, she lifted her hands and slowly began to unbutton the blouse. I said nothing. I sat and watched her.

Her movements were deliberate. She unbuttoned the blouse and pulled it off her shoulders. She dropped it to the floor. Her hands went to the skirt and found the zipper. She removed the skirt, then stood for a moment, motionless, her eyes boring into me; the eyes harboring excitement. I was determined that I would not move.

She reached behind her back. With die lithe, dancer-like motions that always characterized her, she undressed completely. She spread her arms. The light cast deep shadows across the flawless perfection of her body, an aureole glow about the tawny blondness. She stood unmoving, inviting, her head tilted slightly towards me and to one side, the smile of conquest disfiguring her beauty. My hands were knotted into fists in my lap.

"Are you coming to bed?" she asked in a voice that was barely audible.

My stomach churned and a desperate cry of rage gathered and strangled in my chest. I came out of the chair and stood facing her. I slapped her across the face.

The sound was like a shot in the dead silence of the room. Her head snapped back and an expression of surprise and shock replaced the smile. But she did not lift her hands, and she recovered quickly and smiled.

"Are you coming to bed?" she repeated.

I slapped her again. This time she took a step backwards, but she still smiled.

My heart was beating rapidly, and I was weeping inside myself. I had never struck a woman before. It was a complete denial of a code of ethics that had been drilled into me as a child; a negation of my environment. A man, in order to survive as a distinct personality, must be true to the roots that anchor him and sustain him. Each man is—in effect—but a sequence in a chain of life. While his personality may be the sum of his own experiences, his code of behavior springs from the past and the indelible teachings of his ancestors. I had struck this girl in anger and frustration, and in that instant I slipped from the confines of a tradition. I had performed a cowardly act against a background that decreed: *Above all things, a man must live as a man.* In the short space of a hand traveling through the air and connecting with the flesh and bone of that woman, I had lost something of myself, and I could never again be the same person I had been the moment before. It was a frightening and distressing revelation.

Leslie lifted her arms and held them outstretched to me. "David," she said, as though I had done nothing, "come to bed with me."

"Let me alone," I whispered.

"You want me, David."

"I can't."

"Look at me, David. I'm yours. I only want to be with you."
She spoke the words, but behind each word was a deeper meaning. *I possess you,* she was saying. *I control you through your hungers, your lust, your weakness.*

I wanted to turn away from her at that moment, to leave then with the remains of my failing dignity. But I could not move away from her. I hated her as I loved her, my emotions an admixture of loathing for myself and longing for her. I knew that if I left I would have to crawl back; I knew that I would crawl back, that I would submerge any feeling of pride to be with her.

Stepping forward, I reached for her and lifted her into my arms. Her arms encircled me and she clung tightly. I carried her to the bedroom and put her down upon the bed. She lay there, unmoving, and I undressed.

No words were spoken. I came to the bed and stretched out next to her. We were close, but untouching, holding, talking with our eyes.

A sudden pained expression appeared in her eyes. It was as though she were awakening from a sleep. "David," she said, an edge of panic in her voice, "what have I done to you?"

I closed my eyes and swallowed, unable to speak, an unfathomable misery clutching me.

"Oh, David!"

We came together, a breathless impact of longing. We clung together as though in fear of being lost. My love for her flooded me. The blood throbbed against my temples. She began to cry, softly, quietly, a muted sound of terrible anguish, her body shaking under my touch. "David," she said, "why do I do that? Why?"

I nuzzled the hollows of her neck and kissed her. Her crying ceased as physical desire began to take hold of her senses, blotting out the loneliness and pain. I caressed her body and our mutual passion increased until we were blended in the dizzying paroxysms of physical emotion.

Afterwards, when the jangling nerve endings were numbed, we still clung together, silent now in our new separateness. Then Leslie drifted into sleep and I was alone in the room with my thoughts, my doubts.

I reviewed what Sam had said earlier in the evening, hearing his words with a new perception; I thought about my conversation with Martha, thought about Marion and the children. And against this panorama of people with whom I was involved in one way or another, there was my career as a writer. In a way it all blended in confused patterns. Was Leslie a detriment to my work? She had certainly negated my activity that night. Would I consider marrying Leslie? I shoved this question away from me. It was a stark reality that I did not want to face. Could I ever reconcile my problems with Marion? Never. How much of myself did I owe to my work? All of me, I suppose.

Questions with sketchy, unrealized answers; what every man faces every day of his life in his own way. The simple, insurmountable problems of a man's life. A man travels a straight, predestined path to a hole in the ground. There is no avoiding birth, and with the first awareness of the developed mind, Man realizes that his inevitable goal is the grave. Nothing could be simpler to understand and accept. It is baffling that Man seems to apply his superior intellect towards keeping the period between beginning and end as confused and fouled-up as possible. I really did not know where I was going or why, but I did know that I could not— at the moment—be without the girl who lay beside me.

When I awoke in the morning I was immediately faced with the problem of the unfinished story. I got up and dressed, then I went to the phone and called Dick Berger. It was a difficult thing to do. I didn't like Berger as a person, and he would carry the word to Marion that I was having trouble with my work. I don't know why this bothered me, but it did. I called, made excuses, suffered through Berger's condescension, and got a one-day reprieve. I went into the office and began to work on the story.

I worked through the morning with Leslie coming in for occasional snatches of conversation. She seemed a different person, and I felt that she was genuinely sorry for the scene she had caused the night before. Her cheerfulness was a form of repentance. I felt better about everything. I knocked off for lunch and then went back to it.

In the middle of the afternoon Leslie came into the office. Her attitude was different and she seemed restless.

"Is that story going to take forever?" she asked.

"I'll be done in a few hours," I said.

"I haven't even read it, and I'm bored with the whole thing," she said.

"So am I," I said, "but I need the money."

"I have money," she said. "You don't have to work."

I stared at her. "I'm a writer," I said.

"It takes up too much time," she said, turning and walking the length of the room to the window.

"Men work," I said. "My work happens to be writing."

"It would be more fun if you didn't work," she said. "We don't need the money."

"You forget I have a wife and two children," I said.

She turned and faced me. "I don't forget it," she said. "I think about it a lot. Sometimes I hate them."

"I still have to support them," I said.

"I don't care about that. They take up too much of your time. You're always thinking about them."

It was difficult to know what to say. I was used to Leslie's changing moods, but I had never encountered this naked animosity before. It was obvious that beneath her chagrin was the desire not to share me with anyone or anything; this was basically flattering. But now the division of my loyalties was being challenged.

"They happen to be my children," I said.

"I don't care!" she screamed. "I'm sick of it! Your children, your work! I'm always playing second-fiddle to something!"

I had to remain calm. "That's not true," I said. "I've only mentioned the children once, and—"

"You go to see them!"

"I've been to see them once since I met you," I said.

"And I'll just bet you went up there to sleep with your wife," she snapped.

"Now, wait a minute!"

"It's disgusting!"

"Leslie, what are you—"

"Why don't you divorce her?"

"I—uh—"

"Because you have no intention of divorcing her, because you go up there once a month and jump into bed with her!"

"Let's get off that!" I got up from the chair and crossed the room to her.

"Hit me! Go ahead! You're good at that sort of thing."

"Leslie, for God's sake, what's wrong?"

She grasped the window and slammed it upwards. The afternoon heat poured into the room. She whirled away from the window and stalked away from me. "I'm sick of just being on call," she said.

I didn't answer. Her accusations were too wild, too irrational to be based on any fact. I watched her walk to the desk. She picked up die copy that I had written. With quick movements, she tore the pages in half.

"Leslie!"

She threw the torn pages into the air. "That's what I think of the damned story!"

"Are you out of your mind?"

"Yes, dammit, yes! I'm sick of having you spend your time with everything except me."

"This doesn't make sense. Dammit, I've got to get that story in by tomorrow!" I was angry. I crossed the room and bent down to pick up the scattered pieces of paper. I glanced up.

Leslie went to the typewriter. She grasped it and lifted it from the table.

"What are you—?"

Her face was contorted with anger and the strain of lifting the heavy machine. She staggered with it across the room.

"What are you doing?"

She threw the machine through the open window. "There!" she cried. A moment later it crashed into the courtyard below. "That takes care of that."

I stared at her, horrified by the act of wanton destructiveness, unable to correlate my thinking. It was impossible to identify the girl I had known for a month with the creature by the window. I gathered up the torn papers, folded them and stuffed them in my pocket. I started for the door.

"Where are you going?"

I didn't answer. I was out of the office and into the hallway.

"David!' she screamed. "David, don't go!"

I opened the door and slammed it closed after me. I knew that I had to get away from there. This was too sick. I loved her, there was no doubt of that, but there comes a time when the love has all the properties of a malignant cancer, and that is the time to cure it. I ran down the stairs. I heard the door open behind me.

"David!" she screamed into the hallway, her frenzied voice echoing. "David, don't go! Don't go!"

I closed my mind to the anguished plea in the voice, made myself run. Her voice was a distant, plaintive moan, and then she began to cry. I slowed my steps. A part of me said: *Go back to her. You can't afford to lose this.* I forced myself down the remaining stairs and bolted into the street. I ran for half a block as though I were being pursued. When I reached the corner I slowed to a walk, but I did not stop.

My feelings at that moment were a mixture of fury and self-pity. It was a situation beyond reason. I walked fast. I wanted to cry and there were no tears. I wanted to wail and I did not utter a sound. I was seething with the desire to do violence. I wanted to lash out at something, to destroy. I kept walking. I had been hurt and I wanted to inflict pain in return. I had had an image shattered; I had seen what I did not want to see, and I was furious with this new knowledge. I wanted to wipe out the memory of what had happened in the past day, and knowing that I could not, I snarled and cursed my misfortune. Where was the girl of the first night? God, how could I have been so stupidly blind?

I surged along the street, seeing nothing, hearing nothing. I ignored the insufferable heat. I walked fast, flagellating myself for my soiled dream. It was a terrible revelation. The girl was human.

By the time I reached my apartment I was exhausted, but my anger had also dulled, and now there was only the sense of loss, the disappointment.

Claude came out of his studio when I entered. He was wearing bathing trunks, and he had two paint brushes on his hand. There were smudges of oil paint on his face and body. I dropped into a chair at the kitchen table.

"What's with you?" Claude asked.

"I've been walking hard," I said.

"You look terrible."

"I feel terrible."

"Too damned hot for that sort of thing," he said. "Too hot for anything. How about a beer?"

"Great."

He went to the refrigerator and removed the beer. He opened it, placed a can before me. "'Welcome home," he said.

We drank. The beer was cold and good. I was beat and drenched with sweat. I unbuttoned my shirt and pulled it off. I leaned back and sighed heavily.

"How's Leslie?" Claude asked.

"Ended," I said. "Finished. Kaput."

"Oh?" He was surprised, but he smiled. Then he lifted his beer. "To true love," he said, grinning.

God, it was good to be home, good to just sit in the casual, uncomplicated atmosphere.

"She throw you out?" Claude asked.

"I ran," I said.

He chuckled. "The battles of the sexes," he said.

"When you win you lose."

"Amen."

"You really cut out for good?"

"It has to be," I said. "Everything just went haywire. It's too fouled up. I don't know what happened, but I do know that the whole thing is too screwy to be good."

"Do you think she'll let you off the hook that easy?"

"It's not a matter of that. I left, that's that."

"Well," he said, "it's too bad in a way. I mean you really seemed to be hooked on her."

"I was. I am. But, hell, I suddenly saw the whole thing destroying me as a person."

We drank in silence. I pulled the tom pages from my pocket and spread them on the table.

"Ann and I are going to get married," Claude said.

I looked up to make certain that he was serious. I saw that he was, and that he was waiting for me to say something. I knew the girl, Ann, well, and I liked her. She and Claude had met at a party and their attraction for each other had been immediate. Their situation was typical for New York. They had dated briefly, then slept together at her apartment, and gradually their relationship became an affair. This is an accepted pattern among the New York expatriates.

"I think it's a good idea," I said.

"Do you really? I mean, I'm still a little edgy about it. I guess it's because I've never been married."

I knew that I had to be careful about what I said. I was ten years older than Claude and he reacted to me as though I were an older brother. I knew that out of the shambles of my own marriage he expected me to come up with the pattern for the perfect marriage.

"Well," I said, "you can either get married now or just forget the whole thing before it gets unbearable."

"What do you mean by that?"

"Just what I say. Let me ask you this: Have you and Ann been having little disagreements?"

"Everybody has disagreements," he said.

"But have these arguments come up for odd little reasons that you never seem to understand?"

"Well . . . uh . . . as a matter of fact, Ann has been acting pretty strange."

I laughed. "She's acting like a woman," I said.

"Are you going to give me the double standard bunk?"

"No, I'm not. I'm just saying that Ann has more time to think about the future in terms of herself as a wife and mother. You're more concerned with the future in terms of success as a painter. Both of you are thinking of the future, it's just that her future is dependent on another person."

"You make it sound as though she's working some angle to get me married."

"Not at all. It's just that she cannot be fulfilled as a woman without marriage."

"We could live together."

"Maybe," I said, "although I doubt it. You've both shaken off middle-class morality to a degree, but it is still there."

"That's nonsense. I don't have American problems. You forget, I'm French."

"With a stronger moral sense than any American. If you don't get married now you'll be denying the necessity for continuity in life. It's a basic fact where the relationship between a man and woman are concerned. You must always have movement; the relationship must always be going in some direction. A man and woman meet and are attracted. Each is actually seeking a mate. The preliminary love-making is merely testing for the compatible mate. The next step is the affair, but the relationship cannot stop there or it will be destroyed. It has to go on to marriage, lawful or unlawful. The next step is children and then the marriage of those children and then grandchildren. The mating instinct is only the primary factor in this natural continuity. Now, you and Ann could live together and it would be a marriage, but you would force her to deny her background. And anyway, if you're going to go that far, if you feel that this is right for you both, marry her and alleviate any chance of her feeling guilt. The only reason that she has been acting strangely is that she is beginning to feel the hopelessness of the static quality of the relationship. It must have a future, and she's sensing it."

Claude sat quietly mulling over all that I had said. He nodded finally, then smiled. "It figures," he said. "I was beginning to feel pretty hopeless about it myself."

"It'll work," I said. "She's quite a wonderful girl."

"What bothers me about it," he said, "is that I'm sure that everyone thinks that their marriage is right when they marry, and then so many end up in divorce."

"Because our customs say that we must take the biggest step of our lives in the blindest possible way," I said. "How the hell these rules were ever established is beyond me, but they have been. I'm sure that it has to do with the basic puritanical morality of the American. They absolutely deny the existence of sex, and if they accept it at all, they refuse to admit that it is the natural and basic reason for the attraction between male and female.

If you could get to the root of every divorce, I'm certain that you would find the couple sexually dissatisfied. I never knew a married couple who agreed on everything and I know a few who don't agree on anything, but they make it together in bed, and that overshadows everything else. The magazines, the churches, all the do-good consultants can preach forever about the ways to hold a marriage together; play together, pray together, all nonsense. A marriage is made in bed, and that's that."

"Hear, hear!"

I laughed, but then I sobered. "I mean it. A guy who marries a sweet little virgin is doing about as stupid a thing as a man can do. Good Lord, it's the same as buying an automobile without starting the engine. They call it morality when it's actually complete imbecility."

"I don't feel immoral," he said.

"Well, you are. In the eyes of society you are, and so is Ann and Martha and myself, and just about everyone else you know. And because you are immoral you've got a better than even chance for a successful marriage. The average person in the Midwest could never begin to understand the standard of morality that exists in New York, and it's their loss, because they also deny the natural impulses of mating with their blinders of morality, and that's why they keep the divorce lawyers busy. Agh, I could keep on about this for an hour."

"Go ahead, you look fine when your face gets purple."

We laughed together, then I shuffled the torn pages of the manuscript on the table. "I have to get to work," I said.

Claude stared at the torn pages. "What happened there?" he asked.

"Leslie didn't like it."

"She has definite ways of expressing herself," he said.

"Yeah. Now, get out of here and let me get to work."

"Okay, then I take it you'll be my best-man."

"That, old buddy, will be a pleasure."

He went back to his studio and I went to work. It took me four hours to retype the torn pages. By that time Claude had dressed and left to see Ann, and I was alone. I had a sandwich and beer for dinner, and kept working.

The telephone rang several times, and each time I stopped and waited for the ringing to stop. I had the feeling that it was Leslie and I had to struggle to resist the impulse to answer. It was disturbing to me that I could talk to Claude about love, and morality, and marriage, and the general relationship between man and woman, and still not be able to apply the same rational thinking in my own life. I knew that with Leslie I would retain nothing of myself, but I wanted to be with her; every moment that I spent at the typewriter was an agony of wanting to forget my own existence as a human being and submerge myself in the aura that was her.

But there was a part of my mind that retained its clarity and saw Leslie as a sickness, and kept me from the telephone.

It was after midnight when I completed the story. I was tired, but I also felt relief. The bills were paid for another month. I drank a final beer and went to the bedroom. It was still hot. I lay on the bed in the dark for a long time. I was exhausted, but restless.

I have no idea when I slept, but I was suddenly awakened by the crash of the apartment door being slammed open. My immediate reaction was fright, but I recovered and leaped from the bed. There was a long groan and a body crashed to the floor in the kitchen. I fumbled for the light switch and turned on the bedroom light. It gave me enough light in the kitchen to find the lamp. I turned it on.

"Leslie!"

She was sprawled face-down on the floor. My reaction to her was anger. *Damn her for busting in here, preying on my sympathy to get me back into her self-indulgent net. I would have none of this nonsense. I was through.* I stood over her. "What do you want?" I barked.

"David," she whispered. She turned on her side and lifted her face to the fight. "David, help me."

I caught my breath. "Leslie." My voice was barely audible. "My God, what happened to you?"

"David, help me."

I was unable to move. I could say nothing. Her left eye was swollen closed. Her blonde hair was spattered and matted with blood. The left side of her face was a purple-red bruise, and her jaw was misshapen. Her lips were split and bleeding.

I dropped to my knees and gathered her into my arms. I lifted her and carried her to the bedroom and laid her on the bed. I turned to leave.

"Don't leave me!" she screamed, clawing for me. "David, don't leave me!"

I pressed her back onto the bed. "I have to get some ice and water for your face. I'll only be a minute."

She would not release my arm. "Save me, David. Don't let him hit me again! Don't leave me, David. I love you. I love you, David!"

I held her close to me until she quieted, then I was able to go to the kitchen for water and ice cubes. I came back and washed the blood from her face, then made an ice pack for the side of her face. When the last traces of hysteria had gone I asked, "Leslie, how did this happen?"

Her voice was like that of a little girl. It was strange to hear her whimper. "I'm not sure."

"But you must know."

"I don't know . . . I . . . I didn't do anything."

"Leslie, where did it happen?"

"In the subway."

"The subway?" I could hardly believe it. I glanced up at the clock. It was 3:30 a.m.

"Whereabouts?"

"I was down by the Brooklyn Bridge. I was taking the subway back up-town. A man grabbed me and just began beating me."

"But what were you doing down at the Brooklyn Bridge at this hour? That's *asking* for trouble."

"I don't know. I was just there. I don't know how I got there. Don't ask me anymore questions, David."

A moment later she was asleep. I stood by the bed looking down upon her. Was she telling the truth? There she was, beaten, and I could only think that she was lying; and I knew that I would never be able to believe her again. There would always be doubts, and so long as there was doubt of her veracity, there could be nothing for us. I knew then that she walked in the shadow of violence, that wherever she was there would be the seed of disturbance. In her way she loved me, but her nature decreed that this love must be torn and dragged in the mud as punishment for whatever it was that lurked in the untouchable recesses of her mind. Our love affair had been too constant, too pleasant, and she intentionally created the breech. Could she possibly have gotten herself beat up just to make certain that I would go back to her? It seemed unbelievable, but just the fact that I could think such a thing was reason enough to stay away from her.

But I knew that I would not; that I *could not* for as long as she would want me near her.

I pressed my fingers against my eyes. Where would I end in this?

CHAPTER FIVE

My affair with Leslie had a defined pattern.

In the month following the mysterious beating I came to accept certain facts. Leslie, I was certain, had a definite schizoid personality. She was not acting her various roles. When she was charming and understanding, she meant it and felt it; when she was the complete bitch, she was just that. It is always difficult to accept a mental abberation in a beautiful woman, but I had to force myself to realize that there was a Leslie who loved and needed me, just as there was a Leslie who hated my guts.

It was difficult, but during that month I was able to sense the subtle changes, and I did my best to stay away from the side of her that rebelled against me.

I was able to do my work in a haphazard fashion, managing to get just enough accomplished to keep going. I knew, of course, that something had to give . . . and it did.

If I remember correctly, it was near the end of July. It was mid-morning. I had not seen Leslie for three days. I had been working steadily on my most promising writing assignment to date—the treatment for a low-budget movie. While the pay was not astronomical, it was an assignment that could lead to better things, and I was bearing down on it, anxious to pull it off.

I was finishing coffee when the telephone rang. It was Sam, my agent.

"How goes it, Kid?" he asked.

"Fine," I said. "Just fine."

"You're not crapping me, are you?"

"I mean it. Why would I lie?"

"All writers lie," he said. "That's what makes you writers. You're respectable liars."

"Well, it's going fine," I said.

"That broad leaving you alone?"

"If you're referring to Leslie," I said, annoyed, "I haven't seen her for three days."

There was a moment of silence, then he said, "I hope you're not crapping me, Dave."

When he called me Dave like that I knew that he was really concerned. "You have to trust me," I said.

"You, I trust," he said. "But that broad is bad news. I won't relax until that baby is gone."

"Forget it, Sam. I'm doing the treatment."

"Okay, okay. Just checking. You know how important this thing is."

"Believe me, I know."

"This can be the big one, Kid. For you and for me. I don't get that treatment, I'm dead with Carmine. He's gonna be big, Kid, and we'll have the inside track on all his work."

"It'll be done," I said, beginning to weary of Sam's trepidation.

"Tomorrow morning, right? We got a meeting for ten o'clock, right?"

"It will be finished. It will be good." I emphasized each word.

"Okay, okay, don't get sore. It's you I'm thinking about. I'm your agent, you know."

"I know."

"Okay, I'll let you get back to work. Goodbye."

"Goodbye, Sam." I waited for his click, then hung up the phone. I finished the coffee, and went back to the typewriter.

The day went slowly. It was hot in the apartment and I was working in my shorts. Claude had gone to the Cape for the week, so it was as quiet as a building can be in the Lower East Side. The sweat ran. I drank orange juice, and every damned sip made me think of Marion. *The vitamin C will keep you going.* Christ, couldn't I ever do anything on my own? I paced, I sweated, I worked. There were those moments when I knew with clarity that the movie would be a piece of garbage, that what I was sweating to put into words would then result in the labor of a hundred pages of more words, and then the group labors of dozens of technicians and actors and the employ of tons of equipment and the use of thousands of feet of expensive film, and all this for the production of a movie designed for the puckered navel mentality of the Great Unwashed. It was distressing to realize the amount of effort that was pouring into the creation of crap, but I managed to shake myself off the self-righteous pedestal by saying over and over again: *Money, money, money, money.* And I followed this with: *Shit, shit, shit.* But I was able to keep working.

The phone rang. I ignored it. It persisted. I answered it.

"Were you sleeping?" Leslie said.

"Working," I answered.

"Still?"

"Still. It's going good."

"I haven't seen you for days," she said. I noted the slight petulance in her voice. "Will I see you today?"

"I can't," I said. "I have to finish this thing."

She sighed deeply and I got the danger signal. "Well," she said, "I just wanted to know. There's an old friend in town, and I guess I'll have dinner with her."

I felt relief. No scene, no recriminations. I was off the hook. "I'll call you as soon as I'm done," I said. "It really is important."

"I'm sure it is," she said. "Well, work good."

I was about to say more, something sentimental, about how much I missed her, something, but she hung up and I didn't have the chance. I stood holding the phone, staring at is as if I could learn something from it. Was she angry? Dammit, why did it bother me? She had moods. I accepted this fact. She was as nutty as a Mars bar. Then why did it bother me?

I went back to work with less relish than before. She kept getting in the way of my thoughts. What the hell did I want? If she had created a scene on the phone I would have been annoyed, accused her of interfering with my work, and when she accepted the fact that I wasn't going to see her with casual indifference, it still bothered me. Damn!

More orange juice, more sweat, and I was into the fifth draft when I knocked off for a dinner of peanut butter sandwiches. I relaxed by composing an unsolicited testimonial to the inventor of peanut butter, then I picked up my ragged and dogeared copy of Norman Mailer's *Advertisements For Myself.* I read for a half hour, then tossed the book across the room and slumped into the chair, scowling, the dead-weight of conscience nagging me.

Mailer is not for a hack. He says too much, opens up too many windows of the mind, and when you look out you see yourself. I had always known one thing to be an unassailable truth. Every time a man compromises himself, no matter how many excuses he may invent to give his compromise the air of nobility, he loses a little of himself. This is a frightening thing to a writer who started out with a dream of putting something significant into print, a sentence, a paragraph that would raise him above himself; it is frightening when you are 34 and you haven't done it. I could agree with Sam that I was developing in my own way, but in the twilight hours of the heart's hunger I was afraid. I lost something of myself each time I wrote what I knew was trite before I started, and I wondered if there would be anything left of me when I reached that place—wherever it might be—when I *wanted* to put myself into the work.

Mailer on Mailer was an outcry to all writers—I still thought of myself as a writer—to cut out the low whoring and cheating and to be honest unto themselves. He said point-blank that you can't walk through shit without getting the stink on you, and while you may be *tip-toeing* in the gutter, you're still in the gutter.

A writer who whores, he said in effect, is emasculating himself not only as a writer, but as a man.

I mention this because it is important. To read Mailer on the tail-end of a three-day labor on a screen treatment was like pausing for a chat with Christ on the way to a whore house. I was sick with myself. Was this it? I asked myself. Was this my place? Was I merely a word flunkie, the esteemed author of two-syllable imbecility to keep the cameras grinding for a producer with the sensitivity of a gorilla and the brains of gnat?

The dinner break stretched into several hours. I was sitting in the dark. My depression had flowered into a brooding anger. I was no longer merely reviewing the failure of my work, I was also seeing the failure of my life. My weaknesses stood out in the darkened room in technicolor, a leering panorama of cowardice and ant-size insignificance. If I had an ounce of guts I would go dig ditches and write. If I had an ounce of guts I would divorce my wife. I would seize my life and live it.

I turned on the lights and went back to the screen treatment. I cursed Mailer and his book. Later, I said, later. Get this job done and worry about who you are later. Right now you're a hack, so be a good one.

The phone rang and I snarled and knocked the chair over getting up. It was Leslie.

"Hi," she said, too brightly.

"Hello," I said. "How was dinner?"

"Wonderful." She slurred the word. "What are you doing?"

"Sitting here thinking about you," I said.

"Aren't you sweet."

"Are you drunk?"

"Of course I'm drunk," she said. "Beautifully drunk. Wonderfully, beautifully, sensationally drunk."

"That's fine," I said. "Why don't you go to bed and sleep it off."

"I might just do that."

There was music in the background and over this I heard a male voice. I had been depressed, then annoyed that she was calling me drunk, and now the sound of that voice, knowing that she was with a man, infuriated me. I had been feeling mentally cuckolded, and now I was feeling physically cuckolded. It was an unbearably constricted feeling, a type of anger I had never experienced. It was jealousy compounded with fear.

"Is that your friend?" I said.

"What?"

"Your old friend," I said with sarcastic emphasis. "The *she* you were having dinner with. Her voice is awfully deep."

She laughed. "Of course not, silly. That's . . . oh, dear, I've forgotten his name. Just a minute." She spoke away from the phone, asking the man his name, then she came back to me. "It's Murray," she said, "and he's very sweet. He bought me a drink at the Embers, and he says I'm beautiful. He's very nice, and he's a gentleman, and he's not stuffy and working all the time like some people. He bought a beautiful bottle of scotch and we're going to drink it all up."

"Leslie, why don't you cut this out?"

"I don't want to cut it out. I'm sick of just sitting around waiting for you. Goodnight, Mister Big Writer."

The phone clicked and went dead. I took a deep breath, bit down on my lower lip.

I was angry, but more than that, I was afraid. I had to have her.

Don't try to rationalize this, don't ask me why? Someone once told me that it was because of a Christ complex, born of guilt; that I sought atonement for my sins, and Leslie was my cross, and that symbolically, our matings were the spikes being driven into the hands. I don't know, I don't try to explain things in that way. I had to have that damned female, that's all!

For the past two hours I had sat in the sweating self-doubt of my position in life, feeling as necessary as an extra pimple in a field of acne. And now I was about to cuckolded by that impossible, neurotic bitch. Damn women! Damn me for being such a simpering, frightened, ineffectual bastard!

I slammed the telephone receiver upon the cradle. I kicked the fallen chair out of my way and lunged out of the apartment. I ran down the steps, across the courtyard, through the front building and into the street. There were many people on the street, but they did not slow me. I weaved and shouldered through them, running. Voices shouted behind me, but I paid them no heed. I dodged the traffic on Fourteenth Street and cut through the housing project.

It did not occur to me that it would have been simpler to take a cab. The primal rage was upon me. I ran, my anger like a ballooning cancer. It was difficult to breathe. My side ached. My face was contorted. I ran. My feet slapped heavily on the concrete. For long moments of tortured fury I forgot my objective and felt myself pursued, and did not know why I was running away. And, of course, as I ran towards Leslie I *was* running away—from myself, my failure.

I pushed too hard and I had to stop. I clutched the side of a building and gasped for breath. I choked. My senses blurred and nausea gripped me. I retched, spewing the building with vomit. I heaved until the pain was unbearable and the tears ran down my face. I pushed away from the wall and lurched across the sidewalk. People shied from me as though I were a leper. I took great swallows of air and began to run again.

The last two blocks I walked. Suddenly I did not want to rush. I was hesitant to realize the truth of my fears. I reached her building, stopped and looked up. Light showed in the bedroom windows. I used my key to open the downstairs door and climbed the stairs without haste.

I stopped before her door. I held the key in my hand. I waited. My anger seemed to have disappeared. I was chilled and

I was calm—too calm. I slipped my key into the lock, and this was a contradiction, because I turned the key carefully so as not to be heard. One moment I did not want to believe that she would be in bed with the stranger, and now I was trying to catch her unaware. I opened the door and closed it softly. I listened a moment. There was no sound but the record player on low volume. Then I heard Leslie's husky laugh, and suddenly the fury raged in me once more. I walked along the hall at a natural pace. I came into the living room.

They were on the divan. They had heard my footsteps and they regarded me with surprise. The dog trotted over to me and nuzzled my hand. There was a bottle on the table before the divan and two glasses. The bottle was half empty.

"David!" Leslie said, still reclining against the cushions. Her fingers fumbled with the buttons of her blouse, attempting to close it.

The man was still leaning towards her, but his head was turned in my direction. He had a nondescript face, the expense account poached egg look, that faceless face that floats along all the streets of the country. I knew that I had nothing against him, but if I was going to be replaced I wanted it to be by more man than that, so it galled me. He did not say anything, but he registered surprise and confusion.

Leslie struggled to her feet. The initial surprise over, she acted with nonchalance. She weaved just a little, and her voice was a little too stilted. She exaggerated all movement when she was drunk.

"What are you doing here?" she asked. When I did not answer she turned to the man who was now sitting stiffly. "This is my friend," she said. "Murray, this is David."

Murray attempted a weak smile. He was not a happy man. He had picked up a live one in a first rate ginmill, she had all the marks of a sure lay, and now angry young man was on the scene. I couldn't dislike the guy.

"Have a drink," Leslie said.

I crossed the room and stood by the table. I still had not spoken. I looked down at Murray. He was looking back unhappily. "See you around, Pal," I said.

He glanced quickly at Leslie, then back to me. He got to his feet and tried the smile again. "I don't want any trouble," he said.

"You're not going to get any," I said.

He took several steps away. "I don't want to be involved in anything."

"You're not."

"I mean, I just met her," he said.

"I know how it is. See you later." I had control of things now and I was able to ride on his fright.

"She asked me up here." He took another few steps, waiting for me to pull the gun.

"Where you going?" Leslie said, finally reacting to what was happening.

"Murray has a previous engagement," I said, keeping my gaze upon him.

"He does not! He's staying right here! We're having a party!"

"Button your shirt," I said, turning to look at her. She blinked and shook her head. She looked down at the open blouse, and pulled it together, bunched in her fist.

"I'm going," Murray said. "I don't want any trouble. I'm just a quiet, friendly guy."

I nodded. Murray was seeing his name on a police blotter, a tough thing to explain to the boss and the wife. A frightened little man. A big stud if the mare had strayed from the herd, but no challenger for the right to mate. He was more secure in the safe prepaid arms of a whore.

"Don't go!" Leslie shouted. "Don't let him push you around."

"Don't listen to her, Pal," I said. "She likes the sight of blood. Just blow."

"I'm going. Don't worry about me. I don't want any trouble. Christ!"

Leslie's face was twisted with the numbed, uncomprehending look of the booze-fogged brain trying to assimilate, and losing the struggle. But she was coming around fast and her eyes were taking on a glitter. "What is this? What is this?"

"Cool it," I said.

Murray had his hat and was making for the doorway. He gingerly skirted the dog lying by the bar. The whole scene was almost funny.

"Wait just a goddamned minute!" Leslie blurted, and now she had a grasp of the situation. "Don't you leave" she snapped.

Murray stopped dead in his tracks, and I knew who was the boss around his house.

"Just who the hell do you think you are?" Leslie said to me. "You don't own me. You can't come around here messing up my life."

"Stop acting like a two-bit tramp," I said.

"You son-of-a-bitch!"

I hit her. The back of my hand caught her across the right side of her face. Her scream followed the sudden impact. I had put some weight behind it, and she staggered off-balance, hit the edge of the divan and fell to the floor.

Murray was out of it. I heard the door close and the quick rattle of his steps going down the stairs. I could almost hear his sigh of relief, and I knew that before he reached the bottom he would already be editing the story for telling to the next group of salesmen. The American hero.

Leslie was coming to her feet. I started to walk away. She was standing, then suddenly she was on my back and there was a hellish bum as her fingers raked my neck. I whirled, flinging her off. Her eyes burned with fury. She rushed at me. I feinted away and grasped her wrist. I spun her off-balance, shifted my weight and flipped her. She sprawled, but she bounced to her feet with the grace of a cat.

"Cut it out!" I said. "You'll get hurt!"

There were tears of anger in her eyes. She rushed me again. This time I spun her about, holding her arm behind her. I placed my foot against her buttocks and sent her flying harmlessly across the room.

The dog was up and milling nervously. He knew that something was damned wrong, but he was used to me and did not know what to make of it. He whined and barked.

Leslie was leaning against a chest. "I'll kill you!" she screamed. She grabbed a vase and threw it, a wild throw. It shattered against the brick wall. I walked towards the window at the end of the room. "I'll kill you!" she screamed again. I laughed and I shouldn't have, because it triggered her rage beyond reason. She pushed away from the chest and moved to the bar. The dog nuzzled her hand, whimpering. She stood straight, and it was startling to me to see such a beautiful face show so much hatred. She was calm, smouldering. She lifted her right arm and pointed at me.

"Fang!" she snapped. "Get him!"

I caught my breath, stunned with terror by the implication of the harsh order. My muscles stiffened and the fright churned in my stomach. It was a split-second reaction, just as much time as it took the big Doberman to register the order. That was a highly-trained dog and the master had pushed the button that changed me from friend to enemy. I could almost see his muscles coil, and then he leaped from her side.

For a fleeting second I knew that I was going to be torn to shreds, but I had no intention of going out easy. I dropped to a crouch, fists out at my sides. I held my breath, muttering to myself, *Come on, you son-of-a-bitch.*

The dog attacked, a snarling black streak. I hated to put my life on the line with something I had read by Carl Akeley about his African adventures and a particular encounter with a leopard, but there was nothing else I could do.

I gauged the animal's strides, and in that instant that he left the floor to go at my throat, I turned, bracing myself to take the blow on my back. The dog landed, jarring me, but the animal was surprised and I was not. I twisted, spinning him off. In the moment of his confusion I slammed him across the nose. He backed off a step and snarled. The teeth were bared. He bunched up and leaped, but just before he left the floor I stepped in, my fist cocked. His mouth was open wide, but he was off target, knew it too late. I aimed perfectly and slammed the fist into his mouth and down his throat. Before he touched the ground I swung my free arm under his chest, holding his front feet off the floor, and hugged him to me, keeping the fist lodged in his throat.

The animal went crazy. He could not bite down, but he writhed and jerked, kicking with his powerful hind legs. I could only compare it to the first time—at Air Force gunnery school—that I had stood up behind a swivel-mounted twin-.50 machine gun, gripped the handles tightly and pressed the triggers. But, at least the wildly bucking gun was not trying to devour me.

I held on, bent over, my legs spread wide. My face was close to the dogs. He was strangling and I saw the panic and new terror in his eyes. *Die, you bastard!* I gasped to myself, straining every muscle to hold on.

"You're killing him!" Leslie screamed. "You're killing him!"

I glanced up. She was still standing at the end of the room. Both fists were clutched at her throat. She leaned slighdy forward and her face was a picture of anguish.

The dog was losing strength. The strain was telling on my muscles. The dog's eyes were beginning to bug. I thrust the fist deeper.

"Don't!" Leslie wailed. "Don't kill him!" I watched her fall to her knees and begin to beat the floor with her fists. She lifted her face. The expression was tortured and tears streamed over her cheeks. "He's . . . all . . . I . . . have!"

I jerked my fist free and flung the animal away from me. Leslie gasped, leaned forward on her hands and knees, poised expectantly. The dog scrabbled about, gasping for air. He lunged to his feet, staggered and fell. But in a moment he was up again, and this time he came at me. I had to admire the relentless courage, but it was my fight by then, and I was tired of the crap. I hooked a right to the dog's jaw. The animal yelped and fell back on his haunches.

"Come on, you bastard!" I snarled. I advanced a step and hit him again. He backed off, confused and frightened. I hit him again.

"Stop it!" Leslie screamed. "Stop it!" She was still on her hands and knees.

I cocked my fist again and this time the dog dropped to his belly and groveled, whimpering.

"Stop it!"

"Maybe you'd like it!"

"Yes! Yes! I don't care, but don't hit him!"

I crossed the room and stood over her, looking down. She lowered her head. I dug my fingers into her hair and jerked her face up. "Look at me, you goddamned miserable little bitch!" I looked down into the nightmare behind her eyes. "That damned dog would have killed me!" I still held her hair and I shook her head. I shouted about the dog, but my real anger sprang from my soul-sick sense of loss; she was gone from me. I wanted to beat her into loving me. "Why? Dammit, why?" She did not answer. I had lost her, I loved her. I took my hand from her hair and slapped her across the face. "Tramp!" I snarled. "Damned whore!" Her expression had not changed. "I love you, damn you!" I shouted. She covered her face with her hands. "Why, dammit?" I repeated. "Why did you turn that dog on me?" I punished her with the words and I wanted to take her into my arms. "Goddamn you, answer me!"

"I don't know," she said, her voice muffled by her hands. "I don't know." A tight sob choked off anything else.

I stood away from her. I looked down upon her and I ached with longing for her. "You're not worth the space you take up on that floor," I said. "You deliberately called me to get that poor guy beat up tonight. You damned near got that dog killed. Why? What makes you think you're worth all that?"

She pulled her hands away from her face and I winced at the look of hopeless, terrified agony. She opened her mouth to speak, her lips moved, but it was several seconds before she could say, "I . . . I . . ." She shook her head wildly. "Oh, my God!" she moaned. "Oh, my God!" She twisted to one side and sprang to her feet. She held one hand to her mouth, her head down, and ran into the hallway. She ran into the bathroom and slammed the door. I followed, walking slowly. I stood by the door.

A bottle clattered against the metal of the medicine cabinet, fell to the floor. I cocked my head, wondering. I heard her gasp. My heart-beat raced with the nerve-numbing new panic. I held my breath. "No," I whispered. I slammed against the door. It was not locked and it flew open. I stumbled into the room.

Leslie leaned over the bathtub. One wrist was bleeding and she held a razor blade poised to slash the other. I lunged for her and grasped both arms. She screamed and fought to free herself. "Let me go!" she screamed. "Let me go! I don't want this!"

"Stop it!"

"No! Leave me alone!"

"I'll have to hit you!"

"Let me be!" She twisted and squirmed, tried to slam me with her head. I worked my hand around her left arm until my thumb was near the armpit. I found the artery and pressed it tightly against the bone.

"Leslie, you little idiot, stop it."

Gradually I quieted her. She settled into a lethargy of despair. I was able to release one arm and remove the razor blade from her fingers. I held the left arm in both hands and released the pressure on the artery. She watched with disinterest. The blood flowed again, but it was not arterial.

"It's not deep," I said. "You'll be all right."

"I couldn't even do that right," she said.

"Leslie," I said, "don't talk like that. It was my fault and I'm sorry."

She said nothing more. I put her wrist under the water tap and washed the blood away. I probed the wound with my fingers. It was not deep enough to require stitches. I cleaned it with alcohol and bandaged it. She sat through it all like a sleepwalker.

I led her out of the bathroom to the bedroom. She sat on the edge of the bed. "Feel better?" I asked. She nodded without answering. I went to the chair and sat down facing her.

"I told you not to love me," she said.

"What?"

"That first time," she said. Her voice was weary, a dull monotone. She stared at the wall ahead of her. Her shoulders were slumped. "That was so long ago," she went on. "I told you not to love me.

"Leslie, don't—"

"What's wrong with me, David?"

"There's nothing wrong with—"

"Yes, there is," she said emphatically. "I do these things and I don't know why." She looked up at me. "You should just let me die, David."

"That's pretty selfish," I said. "You don't seem to realize that part of me would die with you. I want you, Leslie. I need you."

She stared at me and our eyes held for a long moment. She swallowed and I watched her eyes fill with tears. We said nothing, but the pull between us was strong.

I got up from the chair and went to the bed. I put my hands upon her shoulders and pressed her back upon the bed, lying beside her. I kissed her gently, but she received the kiss hungrily and pulled me to her, clinging with a trembling desperation.

We parted and our eyes held. We said nothing, but we both stood and undressed. We returned to the bed. We were side-by-side, not touching, silent, letting the feeling that was in both of us communicate. I reached out and placed my hand on her arm. The move was timorous, exploratory. She moved closer and our bodies touched. It was difficult to breathe. We came together with the ardent expectancy of first mating. Tenderness gave way to the pure physical desire that was like a hard fist in the guts. This love bloomed in the bowels and spread white-hot through the body. There were no words of love. Our breathing was sharp and tense. Arms and legs clutched and intertwined. Our bodies ground together. Every sense was sharpened and brought into play, touch, smell, taste—everything building towards the intensification of this lust.

I opened my eyes to look upon her face. She grimaced, her teeth bared, and she shook her head from side to side as the need for release enveloped her.

In that moment I decided to master her. My brain seemed to take over and my body calmed. I made love to her methodically, sensing her through movement, watching her face. I brought her near to climax, then carefully calmed her; brought her back again, stopped her, soothed her. When she could not stand it I let her ride over the crest, but minutes later I aroused her again, brought her to the crest and eased her over. I repeated this again, and then she was staring up at me with fatigued eyes. Her look was confused, but I smiled down upon her, saying nothing, and began to slowly, carefully stroke her body. She knew, it was in her eyes. I was using her, but there was nothing that she could do about it. Her nervous system was in control of her and I played upon that nervous system. I moved against her, stroking her, kissing her, until she once again twisted and lunged towards fulfillment, and then I began to speak into her ear, whispering intensely, coaxing her, uttering the guttural sounds of passion, adding the sense of hearing, telling her, "Now! Now, baby, now!" Telling her in those terse bombarding words that all before had been anti-climactic. She twisted and writhed beneath me. Her mouth was open, gasping, and her eyes were begging. I ruled her. Exalted, I grasped her, and released my body from my mind.

Strangled sound rattled in her throat. She kicked her legs. Her heels dug in and she arched her body. A piercing scream exploded from her. I glanced at her face. Her eyes were wide and they rolled back into her head until only the whites were exposed. I shuddered with convulsive spasms. For a long moment we soared into the fourth dimension of time and space, weightless, disembodied. Then we collapsed together, returned to exhausted reality. We lay unmoving, wordless, the sweat cooling on our bodies.

I had won. I had lost. It served my ego to know that no other man had brought her to that point before, that no matter with whom she made love in the future it would be a failure, that there would always be the subconscious remembrance of this night. But I had also reduced her for myself, and knew that the only thing that would bind us now would be this compulsive mating. I have said before that a relationship between man and woman is welded in bed, that the physical mating must be strong and reciprocal. But I must add; when there is nothing else, when a man and woman exist for each other only in the hot sweat of lunging bodies, it is dual masturbation.

I slept and was awakened by the ringing of the telephone. I glanced at Leslie, but she did not stir, so I left the bed and answered it.

"David?" It was Sam. My pulse leaped and I turned quickly to look at the clock. It was almost ten o'clock.

"Yes," I said, my stomach churning.

"I been trying to get you," he said. "You sound like you just woke up. I might have known you'd be with that damned broad."

"Look, Sam, I—"

"Ten o'clock," he said, interrupting. "I told you ten o'clock. You got that thing finished?"

I paused too long with my answer and I heard him muttering curses away from the phone. "I have an unpolished draft, but it ought to—"

"Balls!" he growled. "That broad, that damned broad! I counted on you for this."

"I've got—"

"You've got nothing!" he shouted. "This isn't a two-bit piece of crap for a girlie book, this meant some real dough. You blew it, boy, you did it good. I've had it! You can get yourself a new agent!"

"Sam, look, just give—"

"I've had it!" he shouted. "Go back to bed, lover, and this time you better put the boots to that tramp, because it's going to be the most expensive lay you ever had." He slammed the phone down.

I stared at the dead instrument in my hand. I replaced it in the cradle and stood there clenching and unclenching my fists. I had loused up again and I was boiling with self-pity and loathing for myself. If there was one bit of pride that I had always had in myself as a writer, it was the knowledge that I was a real pro; I could be depended upon to produce damned near anything. I was cautious not to let this become an end in itself, but it had sustained me. And now I didn't have that.

In the bathroom I splashed water on my face, then gazed into the mirror, cursing the image. I went back to the bedroom and began to dress.

Leslie stirred. I turned to look at her. She opened her eyes and smiled. "Good morning," she purred, stretching.

I glared at her with vehemence. She lost her smile. I turned away.

"David," she said, "what's wrong?"

"Nothing."

"But there is."

"It's nothing. It has nothing to do with you." I said those words to shade the issue, to avoid a discussion, but as they were spoken I recognized their truth. It had only to do with me. The whole damned thing had nothing to do with anyone but me. I was destroying everything that was me for reasons of my own, and any contributing factors—Leslie included—were merely catalysts in this willful self-destruction. But, of course, this realization did not stop me. It never does.

CHAPTER SIX

T wo weeks later I saw Marion again.

She had called me and insisted that I meet her in New York. There was an urgency in her voice that I could not deny, and I agreed.

We met for lunch at Costello's on Third Avenue. I was there first, standing at the bar when she came in. I saw her in the mirror. She paused inside the doorway. I did not move for a moment, but stared at her image, viewing her with detachment.

She was an attractive picture. Her dark hair was cropped and curled close to her head. She was not as striking as Leslie, and she did not have the conscious flair of most New York women, but she dressed and carried herself with the self-assured air of the suburban wife.

I turned from the bar. She saw me, relief and recognition lighted her face. She smiled and came towards me. "Hi," she said, "my train was late."

Her smile, her greeting, everything about her put me on the defensive. The attitude of meeting a date was a little much. I said, "Nice to see you."

A white glove fluttered to her face and she brushed aside a strand of hair. "Warm today," she said.

I signaled the head waiter. He nodded and I led her to a table in the rear. When we were seated she ordered a gin and tonic. I asked for my usual beer. The waiter left. Marion looked about her, taking in the dark wood-paneled walls, the collection of junk hanging behind the bar, the original Thurber drawings, the musical chatter of the lunch crowd. She smiled, obviously pleased. "We haven't done this for ages," she said.

I had been prepared to counter her punch for punch, but she was feinting, it wasn't her usual style; I was thrown off balance, but I was wary.

"How are the kids?" I asked.

Her face clouded, but she brightened quickly and said, "Oh, they're fine."

The bait was irresistable and I had to fight to ignore it. "That's good," I said.

"They miss you," she said.

"I miss them."

The drinks arrived, ending that line of conversation. We proposed a silent toast and drank.

"God, that tastes good," Marion said. "It's the only nice thing about summer."

I didn't answer. My curiosity was whetted. I knew she had an angle, but I couldn't figure it. I could have asked her point-blank, but I decided to go along with the game.

"I talked to Sam," she said.

"Oh?"

"He told me you weren't with him anymore."

I knew that he had told her a hell of a lot more than that, but I only said, "We had a falling out."

"I was sorry to hear that. You were so close."

"That's the way it crumbles," I said. "He acted as if he owned me."

"It's because he's so fond of you," she said. "He called me. He's worried about you."

"You'll forgive me if I don't appreciate that. He dumped me, I didn't leave him."

"He's sorry about that."

"He told you all about it, I guess."

She looked down at her hands. She nodded. She looked up and there was hurt in her eyes.

"Do you want to talk about her?" I asked.

She shook her head slowly. "No," she said in a low voice.

There was an uncomfortable silence. I reached for a menu for something to do. The waiter came again and we ordered, then we had to come back to us.

"Did Sam ask you to talk some sense into me?" I asked.

"No," she said. "I suggested something like that, but he said that it wouldn't do any good. He said that you would bounce back when you hit the bottom, and that you—like any man—had to fight your demons in your own way."

"Then why did he call?" I was scowling. I didn't like Sam's philosophy.

"He . . . he wanted to know if I needed money."

I was stunned and annoyed. "Just who the hell does he think he is?"

"He's a friend," Marion said, her voice hardening slightly.

"Of yours," I said.

"Yes. And yours too."

"Some friend. I'm capable of supporting my own family." That was a lie, but the old puritanism was up waving the flag of male superiority.

"He knows that. It's just that he didn't know how you were doing."

"He figures I'm starving without him. What crap. It took me one phone call to get a new agent."

"He couldn't be a Sam." There was a deep, deep sincerity in her voice that made me pause. I sobered and stared down at my glass. I took a deep breath and sighed.

"No," I said, moved to honesty by die tone of her voice, "it's not Sam."

I looked up and our eyes met and for just an instant time raced back and she was that girl I could talk to until five in the morning, the one who could argue with me on a good level, who could put her finger on my moods, could perceive my thoughts with a glance. Then I sensed that she was feeling sorry for me and I bridled. I was saved from saying something cutting by the arrival of our lunch.

We ate quietly, then, over coffee, I said, "Marion, you didn't come all the way into town to talk about Sam. What's on your mind?"

She stared, then looked down at her coffee. She looked up, took a deep breath, and said, "I want you to come back."

I was shaking my head even before the statement fully registered. "It wouldn't work," I said.

"You could try."

"It won't work, Marion."

"I'll make it work."

"No, we've tried it and tried it."

"I came here prepared to beg," she said.

I passed a hand over my eyes. "I wish you wouldn't," I said. "I don't feel good about this, believe me, but it just won't work."

"Why? Why won't you try?"

"Marion, I've told you before. I don't love you. I'm sorry, but I don't. I like you. I respect you. And that's why I can't live with you. It's a lie. Every minute I act like a husband towards you I am insulting you, because I don't believe it or feel it. If I didn't like you it might be different, but I can't cheat someone I respect. Have you any idea what I go through every night when I'm with you? It nears the time that sooner or later we have to go to bed, and I get nervous. I know that I'm not going to sleep with you, but I also know that you'd like to be slept with. I know that I'm going to have to turn my back on you, insult you once more as a woman. It bugs me because I know that you're just waiting. And if I did sleep with you, just went through the motions, I'd feel worse. I'd be making a whore out of you, and I can't do that."

"You won't have to come near me, I promise you that," she said.

"But you'd welcome it if I did," I said. She made no answer and it was answer enough. "You see? I'd still be turning my back on you."

"You're turning your back on me now," she said. "Just because you live in New York doesn't change that."

"I know that, but I don't have to live with it. That's selfish, perhaps, but I'm not a masochist."

"David, it's not merely for myself. The children need their Father."

"I'm sorry."

"You owe them something, David. They're your flesh and blood. You created them."

"I know that I owe them something, Marion, you don't have to tell me that. I think about it enough. But do you really think that it would do them a damned bit of good if I were living there against my will? Don't you realize that they would sense that I was martyring myself in their behalf? And don't you think that it would do them a hell of a lot more harm when they realized that their parents were merely tolerating one another to keep up appearances?"

"They need your love, David."

"And they've got it. For God's sake, Marion, I know that I'm a failure as a parent. But that has nothing to do with loving my children. Being with them doesn't mean that I will love them more."

"But you'll lose them, David."

"I don't think so. I don't know, I may be wrong, but I don't think I will. I do know that if I lived in that house there is a better than even chance that they will learn to hate me. What I am doing now is honest, at least, and if they have any feeling when they grow up, they will understand it."

"David, I'm thinking about them *now*. What happens to them now can warp their lives forever. Make them feel wanted, David. Now, make them feel that their Father wants them now."

"And have them hate me later?"

"Yes," she said, "yes. You owe them that. They are *your* children, *your* genes, *your* cells, *your* blood. They are your life after you and it is your responsibility to yourself to sustain the continuance of that life, even if you have to give up your own life in the process."

"I can't."

"You mean, you won't."

"All right, then, I won't. Marion, the psychoanalysts are kept in business by people whose troubles can be traced right back to what you want to create. This way they won't feel that I don't want them unless you make them feel that way, and I know that you wouldn't do that. If I'm going to do them any good it will be by staying away from that house."

She didn't answer. She slipped into a posture of defeat. I felt like hell. I wanted this ended. I wanted to get away from there. Right or wrong, I had made up my mind.

"It's that girl," she said.

"It has nothing to do with any girl," I said.

"Sam told me about her."

"I know that."

"He said that she's hurting you, that she's no good."

"That's a matter of opinion, and Sam doesn't know her. I don't think you'd like her."

"On the contrary, David, I might admire her. I couldn't possibly like her because she has you, but I could probably admire her. It takes a certain amount of courage to be the *other* woman. If she knows you at all, she must know that she will never marry you, because you will never get a divorce. So, she has to deny many of the basic instincts of woman. Her nest is temporary, at best; she cannot legitimately have children by you; the unknown wife is always a threat to her. She has to give up the future, and the number of fortune tellers and astrologists certainly bear testimony to a woman's instinctive interest in longevity and the future. I'm sure that you'll agree that the average working man would not be insurance poor if women were not compelled by nature to think in terms of future stability. She has you, David, but she can never be certain that she will have you for a week or a month or a year."

"This has nothing to do with—"

"But it does, David." She was on her intellectual plane, calculating, unemotional. "I want you to come back to us. I accept the fact that I cannot arouse physical passion in you, and this would not be a part of our life. I want you to come and be a father to your children. I also want you for myself. I can do without sex; I cannot continue without a man in the house. I want this, and I will accept the obvious drawbacks with it. I am quite prepared to accept this girl as your mistress."

"Are you out of your mind?"

"No, David, I'm not. I'm being logical. This is nothing new. It has been going on for centuries in Europe. I want to protect my family unit, and if I must make concessions, I'll make them."

"I couldn't do it. I couldn't do it to her. Marion, I happen to love this girl."

"Then think of her, David. As a mistress she has a position, a clearly defined status. I would have you legally and she would have you sexually, as she does now."

"It's more than that."

Marion gathered up her gloves and purse. She stood up from her chair. "Is it, David? Are you certain of that?" She turned and walked away.

CHAPTER SEVEN

Claude's wedding party was unforgettable. It had the elements of drama. There were two young people in love, and a crowd of friends eager to wish them well, happy in their happiness; the the families of both, opposed to the marriage, now in a state of frozen-smiled traumatic shock. It was a night of humor, pathos, gaiety, drunkenness and near-tragedy.

The wedding was small. I was Best Man. Leslie did not attend. She was moody, depressed, when I called for her to take her to the party. I asked her what was bothering her.

"Nothing," she said.

"Are you sure?"

"I certainly ought to know," she said curtly.

I shrugged, realizing that she was too moody for conversation, and let it go. We went to the party.

There had been a light rain in the afternoon, but it was still hot, the atmosphere close. The small apartment was already crowded when we arrived. It was warm. The men were in shirt sleeves, ties were pulled aside and collars were open.

A concentrated babble of sound rolled through the open doorways, music and laughter and loud talk and singing and shouts, a blend of high-pitched cacaphonic sound that rose and fell with erratic frenzy.

Leslie stopped as we entered the doorway. My hand was on her arm and I felt her stiffen. I glanced at her face. She was holding her breath and she stared wide-eyed.

Seen objectively, the room resembled a mad house. It was a sea of faces glistening with sweat. The noise was a communal thunder. Faces smiled and laughed, mouths moved without the distinction of individual sound. A trumpet blared from the next room. A girl shrieked above the roar. Hands fluttered, seemingly divorced from bodies.

"Quite a crowd," I said to break into her sudden terror of the human mass.

She smiled, a fleeting, timorous contraction of muscles. "I . . . I . . . don't know if I can take it," she said.

"We won't stay long," I said.

Someone shouted, "There you are!" We were confronted by Carl Sacks, a jazz musician. "Come on in! Jesus, Man, what a scene." He was staring at Leslie. I introduced them. "You need a drink," he said. He took Leslie by the arm and propelled her through the crowd. She glanced back at me, her eyes fearful, but then she was lost in the press of people.

I moved into the room. The heat was unbearable. I struggled to the bedroom and left my coat. I pulled my tie loose and unbuttoned my shirt. I went back into the melee and found a drink.

Claude was pressed into a corner, still in a state of confusion, realizing that he was married, but waiting for some metamorphosis to take place. Ann was on the far side of the room, her face radiant with triumph.

I gulped the drink and refilled the glass. I shouldered my way to Ann and embraced her.

"Big day," I said. "How do you feel?"

"Like a woman," she said.

I smiled and looked towards Claude. "He still doesn't know what has happened," I said.

"Oh, the poor thing," she said. "He's terrified. I almost wish I hadn't done it."

"He'll get over it," I said.

"I hope so." She pressed my arm. "David, when I have a moment I want to thank you for the apartment."

"My pleasure," I said. Claude and I had spent a week painting and cleaning the apartment. I was going to move out when they returned from their wedding trip.

I was pushed out of the way. I finished the drink and got another. I found a spot against a wall and watched the throng. It was the same crowd you would find at a gallery opening on 10th Street, or at the Cedar Bar or at Dillons. They were artists and writers, composers, actors, musicians; most of them young. And their women; some of them talented, most of them just the cockroaches who dog the footsteps of talent, eager to fall on their backs and feel the thrust of future greatness. It was a mixed crowd of white and negro, the democracy of the outcasts.

Sweat ran. Smoke billowed and clung to the low ceiling, a blue-white haze. Shirts were open, hanging free. Hankerchiefs were knotted at necks. The air was strong with the evidence of low-rent cold-water walk-ups, odors free of soap scent or deodorant. It was strong, but in the press of humanity, not unpleasant. It was the heavy musk of man-woman sweat and smoke and whiskey, an earthy, sexual stink.

I listened to the snatches of conversation, the disembodied dialogue:

". . . and he'll never learn to use color. I don't . . ."

"So I said, screw, who needs it."

"I quit the damned job. I get unemployment for five months and I'll be able to paint. It's like a Federal Scholarship."

"—the shots didn't work, so he had to get up the dough for an abortion. Poor bastard."

"Christ, it's hot!"

"—and she wanted to move in. I had a hell of a time getting rid of her."

"—but, Baby, you just can't compare Ginsburg with Robert Frost. I mean, like, you just don't."

I swallowed my drink and turned them off, threw the switch on my mind, turned the dial to mob scene. I had heard it all, all, all; all the crap of the nonconformist conformity, all the squeezings of the liberal sponge minds, the bullshit bleatings of the zero talents; all the talk, talk, talk of the evergreen review rabble; all the psychotic gibble-gabble of the vagina-oriented Bronx bagel-babies with their costume-jewelry pearls of Hunter College wisdom. I turned it off and the collective stupidity made a nice hum.

A bongo exploded in the next room. I shoved away from the wall and pushed towards the booze. The heat and the crowd helped, and I was getting high. I jostled breasts and begged the pardon of stranger-faces with mascara masks dribbling clown-fashion down steaming cheeks; with dark-stained armpits. I passed an up-town statue looking for a hole to crawl into and said hello to Ann's brother, one unhappy square toasting little sister into hell. I found the bottle and shouted, "No ice!", and got no answer, and took my medicine straight. I was getting bombed out of my skull.

Leslie. I had to find Leslie. There was drumming and trumpeting and screaming in the next room. I pushed through the crowd. "Give the ball to Rockne!" I shouted. What a crowd! I never knew Claude had so many friends. I was shoved against a girl, thigh and breast. She said, "Hi," and I said, "Low," and she laughed, and I rested my drink on her shelf of sweating, freckled breast, and she said, "Oh," and I said, "P-Q-R," and she said, "What do you do," and I said, "Seduce girls," and she said, "Always in a crowd?", and I laughed, and I lifted my glass and bent my head to kiss the exposed swell of both salty breasts, and she said, "Hey," and a male voice growled, "What the hell are you doing?", and I said, "Seeing if its a girl," and angry voice said, "Wise guy," and I said, "Farewell." I pushed on and made it through the hallway and into the crowd fringe of the dancing people. I wiped the sweat from my face. I had to blink my eyes into focus. I saw Leslie. She was dancing with a negro painter. I knew him slightly, a one-man integration movement. She was laughing and her body responded to the beat with joy.

The music stopped for a moment and I got to her. I said, "Hi."

She faced me. "Oh," she said, the smile leaving her face, "what happened to you?"

"I got caught," I said. The music started. I took her in my arms and we danced, but she wasn't swinging with it. "What's wrong?"

"Nothing."

"You want to leave?"

She didn't answer, but she stopped dancing and removed my arms. She turned and went over to the negro painter. He glanced at me, then grinned, and took her in his arms. They swung into the beat of the music and the smile was back on her face.

I backed off the floor. Something was bugging her and this was her way of putting me down. I had the feeling that everyone in the room was staring at me. My muscles were tightening and the anger was beginning to flow like a poison, pumping through my system at the insistence of my quickened heartbeat. Bitch! I muttered. I turned and went back to the booze. I drank to extinguish the anger. I wouldn't go back in there. To hell with her. I drank and the room reeled, the smiling faces became grotesque. I pushed my way back to the other room. She wasn't dancing, but she was still standing with the negro—I couldn't think of his name—and he was writing her phone number on a matchbook cover, a party game peculiar to New York. Those matchbook covers deliver premiums that could put Green Stamps out of business. I was making a personal contribution towards integration—and I didn't like it. I caught my breath. Damn her! Damn that impossible bitch!

I have no memory of the next moments. I did nothing outlandish or I would have heard about it. But it was a complete black-out.

I found myself standing on the roof. I have no idea how long I had been there. I know that I must have left the party and walked up the one flight of steps. I was standing close to the twelve-inch ledge that fringed the roof. I stepped back. I was drunk. My mind was functioning clearly, but the body wasn't. I sat down and leaned back against the ledge. I closed my eyes. I did not hear her come onto the roof, but I heard her voice.

"David?" she said tentatively. "David?"

"What?" I said.

She rushed over to me. "David, I was worried. Someone said you were staggering around up here."

"Beat it," I said. "Go back to your spade."

"David, come along now." She reached out and touched my arms.

The contact triggered an incomprehensible rage that burst upon me, enveloped me; I came up from the sitting position, my hands went out and I had her by the throat. She gagged with surprise. I swung her about and bent her over the ledge. I put pressure on my thumbs. I was thinking with absolute clarity and I knew that I was going to kill her. She did not resist. Her body was limp. I wanted to see her die. I leaned over to peer closely at her face. I saw her look of triumph and I jerked my hands away.

I turned and staggered away. I could hear her gasp of breath. I found the stairs and started down. I heard her call, "David!" I ignored it and kept going, clutching the railing for support. "David!" I heard the clatter of her high heels. I reeled into the courtyard. She was at my side. She took my arm and I knocked her hand away. I staggered through the front building and onto the sidewalk. The buildings seemed to tilt and the world reversed itself on its axis. I remember her hands on me and the yellow blur of a cab.

I remember, next, her voice coming to me from a great distance. The words were unintelligible, but gradually they cleared. "David, get up. Come on, now, get up."

My awareness returned. I knew that I was lying on the ground, I could feel the grit with my out-flung hands. I was face down. I did not open my eyes.

"David, get up! You can't lie here." She tugged at my shirt. "David, wake up!"

I breathed deeply and I knew something was wrong. My face was lying in something wet and foul-smelling. My brain was operating at half-speed and it took several seconds to realize that I was sprawled in my own vomit. I raised my head and opened my eyes. I was in a vacant lot.

"David, you're awake. Get up, now."

When had I ever been so drunk? Many times. Plenty times drunk and I had never fallen to the ground to lay in the stink of my frustrated stupidity. How could I get lower than this? I turned my face to look up. Leslie was leaning over me. I coiled my body in a continuing movement, bringing my legs up for leverage, and I swung my right arm. The back of my hand cracked against her mouth. She cried out in pain and surprise and fell backwards. I got to my feet.

She stood three feet from me. The moonlight gave her blonde hair a mysterious glow. The deep shadows accentuated the contours of her body. Her face was raised to the light and her angelic beauty was marred only by the trickle of blood from the corner of her mouth.

"Where are we?" I asked.

"On First Avenue," she said. "You were sick. I had the cab drop us here."

"Got a handkerchief?"

She produced a packet of tissues from her purse. I wiped my face. When I finished I looked at her. "Sorry I hit you," I said.

She did not answer. I used one of the tissues to wipe the blood from her mouth.

"It has nothing to do with you," I said. "I'm really sorry. C'mon, let's go."

We walked across 31st Street and stopped before her building. She climbed the steps and fitted the key to the lock. When she realized that I was still on the sidewalk she turned. "David," she said.

I turned and walked away. "David," she said again. I went on. I heard her say my name once more without raising her voice. I did not stop and I did not look back.

I walked down Second Avenue, the night air cool against me. I was returned from a long trip. I bore the stink of my degradation. Where I had been I had to go. What I had done I had to do. I knew that I walked through the night city with new knowledge. I could not analyze it, but I knew that in some way it would be made known to me. I walked with a strong, sober stride, one of the eight city-bound million, a unit, a single entity lately distracted from the true course of birth to bury-hole; distracted for reasons as yet unknown. I touched upon people during this incident, but cause and effect are judged from point of view, and thus you may have noted that I have examined myself only, leaving the others in one dimension in a field of gray. From Leslie the story would be truthfully different. We are each of us alone in this world. If I have sinned, it has been against myself.

EPILOGUE

This is David Markam.

A young-old man of 37, he walks south on Seventh Avenue in New York City. It has been a difficult day for him and he is tired. Four hours were spent in conference concerning sponsor-required changes in a new TV series; two hours were spent haggling over the movie option for his new book. He wonders if Sam, his agent, really fought hard enough for his price before he backed down.

At Sheridan Square he stops and enters a small coffee shop. He sits at one side of the horseshoe-shaped counter and orders coffee. When it is brought to him he sits stirring it, his thoughts elsewhere.

A man and woman enter and sit at the counter opposite him. He looks up at them. The man is balding and his face is red and flaccid. He is rotund in a conservative gray suit. His hands on the counter are pudgy and he wears a ring on each hand. He has the look of a tired salesman. The woman is younger by twenty years, a blonde. Except for the tired, lackluster eyes, she would be beautiful. David returns his attention to his coffee.

"I gotta go to Washington tomorrow," the man says.

"When will you be back?" the woman asks.

David looks up, startled, remembering that voice. He stares hard at the woman. She looks at him, frowning as she notes his interest, and turns away.

"I'm not certain," the man says. "A few days."

"We have those tickets for the theater," the woman says.

David stares at her, memory bringing her into focus. He leaves his coffee untouched and hurries from the restaurant.

"What's with him?" the man asks.

"I don't know," the woman says.

On the sidewalk, David turns for a last look at her through the window. Leslie, he says to himself. My, God, I remember that voice across the distance of a pillow. She's hardly changed and I didn't know her. He crosses the street enmeshed in thought.

How is it possible to be that intimate with a person and not remember her? He cannot realize that she was too much the catharsis to exist as a woman for him, that as he purged himself of his guilt, she too was purged from his memory. *Christ, I remember everything about her, and I couldn't recognize her.* An ideal has no human form.

He walks east on Washington Place and turns in at the entrance to an apartment building. He takes the elevator to the sixth floor and lets himself into an apartment with his key. A female voice greets him from the kitchen. "Is that you, David?"

"Yes," he says.

A girl enters the room. She is young and dark-haired. Her face has a sloe-eyed, sensual beauty. She wears a sweater and tight slacks that display the generous femininity of her body. She holds a martini in each hand.

"Your wife called," she says. "She said to remind you about the drapery material."

He nods, saying nothing. The girl brings him the martini and he sits on the divan. "Your wife must be a strange one," the girl says. "I can't understand her accepting this kind of relationship so casually."

David does not answer. He stares at the girl. She frowns. "What's wrong? Why are you staring at me like that?"

Will I forget this girl? Will I forget that face, that body that responds to me?

If there is more than the face and body, he will. And justly so. The flesh disintegrates and it is the experience that remains.

My God, doesn't it mean anything? Is there nothing to cling to? Do I retain nothing of this?

The yesterday you is a stranger today. A life is like skipping a flat stone across still water. The stone is air-borne, carried by momentum; it touches briefly, again and again until natural law brings it down and it sinks from sight. What exists are the ripples made upon contact, and they spread and dissipate, and what remains of the flight of the stone is the memory of the ripples. A man is only the total of his experience.

"Say, what's wrong with me?" the girl says.

David laughs. "Nothing," he says. "I was thinking of something else. Come here and sit next to me."

THE END

In those forever ago army days, when I was suspended in the vacuum of middle-class arrogant ignorance, I met an artist, a rebellious giant of incorruptible integrity. He gave me a novel to read—my first—and thus opened a world to me; and a hunger to see, to feel, to understand—to write. In the interim years, while I prowled restlessly in that world, exalting its beauty, damning its injustice, pondering the miracle of its seed, doggedly trying to shape thoughts into words, there was always the hovering shadow of my friend and that booming voice to say: BE HONEST! I have written other books, but this is the first I want him to read. It may not be good, I don't know, but I labored hard upon it; I used no cheap tricks, followed no formula, tried to appease no one. If it is a bad book, it is also an honest book. He'll have to accept that.

to
Bill Scharf
a painter

www.ingramcontent.com/pod-product-compliance
Lightning Source LLC
Chambersburg PA
CBHW030353180626
46812CB00007B/2866